M000189919

ATTRACTING AUBREY

GONE WILD

AVERY FLYNN

AVERY FLYNN

Copyright © 2020 by Avery Flynn

All rights reserved.

No part of this book may be reproduced in any form or by any electronic or mechanical means, including information storage and retrieval systems, without written permission from the author, except for the use of brief quotations in a book review.

Cover by Jersey Girl Designs

ISBN: 978-0-9985320-1-1 (print)

ISBN: 978-0-9985320-0-4 (digital)

ONE

Aubrey Dean was a pants thief and she had no regrets.

Now, she wasn't taking just anyone's pants or using the five finger discount in a store. No, she was digging through a suitcase in the hallway of a cruise ship. And it wasn't some stranger's suitcase. The unassuming black suitcase without a snag or a scratch or a speck of dirt on it belonged to one of Aubrey's besties from college.

Grace—said suitcase's corporate-down-to-her-sensible-shoes owner—was smart, amazing, and in desperate need of letting her thighs air out.

When Grace let slip to Aubrey, Kendall, Benjamin, and Liv as they were boarding that she hadn't packed any shorts because of her not-fit-for-public thighs, Aubrey knew exactly what needed to happen. One quick communication spree via knowing looks between friends later and the rest of her old college crew were buying Grace another cocktail while Aubrey went sprinting toward Grace's room. Luckily, she hadn't gotten down to her room yet and her suitcases were still in the hall right outside her door where the porters had placed them.

Really, Aubrey was doing the Lord's work here and freeing Grace's thighs, which had remained covered for pretty much her entire life after her mom had told her they were not the kind of thighs that should ever be seen in public. Yeah, Grace's mom was a judgy bitch. Grace had great thighs—and even if she didn't it didn't matter, no one should spend a seven-day cruise to the Bahamas sweating it out because her thighs were covered the entire time. An intervention was necessary.

Which is exactly why she was giving Grace a friendly little nudge in the be-yourself-and-tell-whoever-doesn't-like-it-to-fuck-off direction. Stealing every pair of pants Grace had brought with her for the cruise was the perfect solution. Okay, maybe not *perfect* but desperate times called for desperate measures.

Aubrey swiped a pair of pants from the open suitcase and extended her arm up in the air. "Free Grace's sexy thighs!"

She was The Thigh Avenger and it felt good.

For the first time in a year, Aubrey was free from the stifling confines of small town life where everyone knew everyone and everything about each other. Even if she was popping motion sickness pills like candy and chasing them down with overpriced tropical drinks, she was going to enjoy every single second of this cruise with her besties from college.

Kendall, Grace, Benjamin, and Liv were the people who knew her as Aubrey Dean: Wild Woman. In small town Salvation, she was deceased Ashley's poor daughter and Marie's troublesome granddaughter.

Her friends expected to see her in crop tops and shorts,

leading the party. Back home everyone in town knew to find her behind the counter at the family bakery covered in flour after another failed attempt at making anything edible.

Here, on board, she could be fun, flirty, and fabulous. In her one-stop-light town, she would always be a never-reached-her-potential disappointment.

Damn, she missed being the woman her friends knew. Small town living had sucked all of it out of her, though—especially when she was reminded almost daily of the Grand Canyon-sized chasm between how she'd planned for her life to turn out and how it actually had. If it hadn't been for her countdown to this cruise and her anonymous Insta account documenting the many, many beautiful photos of Carter Hayes (AKA America's favorite movie superhero The Admiral), she wasn't sure if she'd still be even kinda close to sane.

"Do you need help getting your bag into your room?"

Aubrey started at the man's voice, practically jumping up from her squatting position next to the opened suitcase. "It's not mine."

Way to go, Dean. You're a fucking genius pants thief.

And that was most definitely the wrong thing to say judging by the guy's Boy Scout appearance with his tightly cropped blond hair, square-framed glasses, clean-shaven square jaw, crisp khaki shorts, and totally unwrinkled Hawaiian shirt buttoned all the way up to his neck. Under different circumstances all she would be thinking about was how to dirty him up, but this wasn't the time for that. Later? Oh yeah, she'd be having thoughts, all sorts of naughty thoughts.

"So you're stealing," he paused looking over the small pile next to her, "pants?"

Okay, he hadn't used an old-fashioned police whistle or

made a citizen's arrest, she could still get out of this. She pasted on her sweetest, most innocent smile that usually fooled .2 percent of the population. What could she say, she'd always had a trouble streak and it had always shown through.

"Yes, but I have a good reason." She leaned in close, hoping to make him feel as if he was in her circle of trust. "They're my friend's."

His eyes—a startling shade of blue that seemed way too familiar—narrowed. "It's a prank?"

"Sorta, yeah, let's go with that." Really it was a mission from the higher sexy thighs power but explaining that to the Boy Scout would probably break his sweet little brain.

He crossed his arms over his chest, the move making the seams of his shirt sleeves practically cry out in pain they were straining so hard not to rip under the strain of some seriously drool-worthy biceps. "I don't—"

"Why are you walking so slowly, Kendall?" Grace's voice carried down the hall. "Are you sure you feel okay?"

Shit.

In a move quick enough to qualify for the running-from-killer-clowns levels of fast, Aubrey bent down and picked up the pile of pants and shoved them into the Boy Scout's arms. "Hold these."

Adrenaline spiking, she squatted back down and zipped the suitcase closed and sat it up again like it had been before.

"Why am I the only one worried about Aubrey taking off?" Grace asked, well-deserved suspicion in her tone. "What are you guys up to?"

"Nothing," Liv said, not giving away even a hint that shenanigans were afoot.

"You know Aubrey, she's always up to something,"

Benjamin said. "She's probably already spotted her man of the cruise and is putting him under her spell."

Oh yeah, there was only one guy she wanted to do her bidding right now and that was the Boy Scout. She grabbed him by the arm and hauled him down the hall. "Come on. We have to hustle."

Okay, there was more bulk to him than she'd expected, going by his I-iron-my-underwear appearance, and she had no doubt she was only getting him down the hall by force of personality and not any actual muscles on her part.

"Where are we going?" he asked.

Where? Crap. That was a great question. She glanced over at the number of the rooms as they fast walked without looking like they were getting the fuck out of there, it was only ten rooms shy of hers. All wasn't lost. They could make it.

"We're going to my room."

He stopped dead. "I'm not sure that's—"

"Wait, is that her?" Grace asked before calling out, "Aubrey, I know that's you."

Fuck.

She didn't turn and she didn't slow down. She tightened her grip on the Boy Scout's not-of-this-earth solid bicep under the obnoxious Hawaiian shirt decorated with wiener dogs in grass skirts and kept moving—or at least she tried to. He kept his feet planted where they were and short of using a Mack Truck to shove him forward, she wasn't going to be able to move him.

"Are those your friends?"

She nodded. "Yep."

The first hint of a sexy smirk transformed him from saint to sinner. "So I could blow this thing right now?"

She gave him a sideways glare and prayed her panties didn't go up in flames. "Don't even."

"Aubrey Dean," Grace said from only a few feet behind them. "What are you up to?"

Okay, she knew that tone from Grace. There was no getting out of this. Stopping, she whispered, "Stuff them down your shirt."

His blue eyes rounded behind his Clark Kent glasses. "Why would I do that?"

Good gravy. Did he not understand the time pressure they were under?

"Because if you don't she's going to know they're missing and she can't know that yet," she said. "Grace knows what I look like so I can't put them down my shirt. However, she doesn't know you, so it will just look like you've got a gut. Come on." She gave up on the sweet smile and went straight for damsel in distress desperation. "Do me a solid, please."

This was beyond a doubt the weirdest experience Carter Hayes had ever had and he'd once spent six hours on a green screen sound stage wearing a CGI suit and pretending to fight a one-eyed zombie giant with poisonous farts.

When he'd turned the corner and found the cute blonde giggling to herself as she pulled one pair of pants after another out of a suitcase, he thought she might be a little touched, as his grandmother used to say. When she held one pair up in the air and declared she was freeing Grace's sexy thighs, he figured she was drunk already. And just when he thought it couldn't get more bizarre, she managed to pull him in as an accessory to pants theft and now she wanted him to shove four pairs of pants down his shirt?

This was a mistake. It would only draw attention to himself when he was supposed to be observing others, not be observed. The last thing he needed was for anyone to realize that he *wasn't* mild mannered dental laboratory technician Carter Van Stettle from Iowa. This cruise was his opportunity to prove to indie-darling director Allyson Hernandez that he could disappear into a part, that movie goers could look up at the big screen and see him as anyone other than The Admiral.

He was all ready to return the pants to their rightful owner and be on his way. It was the smart thing to do. Then, the thief beside him said please, and well, one could only play the most debonair superhero to ever top the box office for so long before some of the character stuck to them. He stuffed the stupid pants up his shirt and tucked the hem of it into his shorts to keep them from falling out. The special effects team on his last movie would have laughed their asses off, but the pants' paunch effect was actually pretty good.

"Grace," Aubrey said, turning to face her friends. "I didn't hear you."

Her friend didn't bother to hide her skepticism. Behind her a man and two women were trying not to grin and failing.

He held out his hand. "Carter Van Steetle from Iowa."

"Grace Kim." She shook his hand.

By then, her other friends had gotten control over themselves—obviously they'd been in on the stealing pants prank—and everyone introduced themselves.

"So what are you two up to?" Liv asked.

"Poor Carter got lost." Aubrey gave him a poor puppy

look and hooked her arm through his. "Can you believe he's never been outside of Iowa? This is all pretty overwhelming for him."

Oh, that's how she wanted to play this? The woman with the soft Southern accent that definitely came out more country than old money was calling him a hick? He'd grown up in L.A. the son of movie stars of the multiple Academy Award winning variety, the closest he'd ever been to the country life had been going on set with his parents when they'd shot a movie in Idaho and his annual weekly visit with relatives in Iowa during the summers when he was growing up. Still, he'd been given his part and like any good improv player, he was going to lean into it—with a twist.

"Thank goodness I ran into Andie, here," he said, adding some more yokel to his words. "She just saved me from feeling as out of place as an outhouse in the White House."

"Aubrey," she corrected, looking at him as if she'd never seen him before.

"That's right." He tapped her on the tip of her button nose as she all but growled at him. "She just talks so fast it's kind of hard for my country boy ears to keep up."

Benjamin chuckled. "That's interesting considering she's from a blink-and-you-miss-it small town in Virginia."

"Really? I'm surprised." He turned to face Aubrey, giving himself a second to take her in. She was cute, but in a main-character's-sweet-best-friend-who-fell-for-everything kind of way with her girl next door sensibility betrayed only by her eyes. Those big brown eyes sparkled with trouble. It wasn't overt but it was just enough of a combo of sugar and spice to make him want to know more. Plus, he'd caught her stealing pants; there was definitely something more to Aubrey Dean than her aw-shucks face promised. "You have fast talker written all over you."

She narrowed her eyes at him, not missing the dig at her underhanded antics earlier. Then, as if she'd flipped a switch, she turned the sugar back on and focused on her friends.

"I'll meet you guys back up on deck for the mandatory safety briefing thing." She side stepped closer to him, the strawberry scent of her shampoo teasing him. "I'm just gonna make sure Carter doesn't get lost again."

They turned—meaning she pivoted and he followed along because he couldn't seem to help it with her—and started back down the hall.

The got a few doors down from her friends before she broke the silence. "So where is your room?"

"Eight doors down on the right." Normally he'd be several decks up in one of the full suites, but he'd gotten his assistant to dial back to a more affordable regular room with a balcony.

"Are you kidding me?"

He shook his head. "No."

"We're next door neighbors." She didn't sound very thrilled about it.

What was that all about? It wasn't like he was the one who'd asked to be part of the pants crime of the century. "Seems only right since you've involved me in your life of crime."

She let out a full-tilt snort of oh-yeah-buddy-suuuuuuure. "I wish I lived anything close to that exciting of a life. I own a bakery. Well, it's my name on the business license, but really it's my gran's bakery."

Carbs. He was going to eat so much sugar while he was on the cruise it would make his trainer for The Admiral movies cry. Totally worth it. "So what's your baking specialty?"

"Mine?" She laughed, it was light and soft and too utterly practiced to be sincere. "Nothing. I am whatever a gardening black thumb is to baking. The shop, however, is famous for its bear claws. So will you be using your newfound skills of skulduggery when you return home to Iowa?"

It was a deft turn to get the conversation away from herself and back on him. Damn, he could take lessons from this woman. Diversionary tactics were the best way to maintain a cover according to one of the British secret agents he'd shadowed for an action flick a few years ago. He'd never seen it used in a real life situation though and had it be as smooth as what she'd just done.

"Doubtful they'll be a call for any flim flam," he said, echoing her old timey turn of phrase. "There's just not much call for subterfuge when you fabricate teeth."

"Like dentures?"

Thank God his cousin, who actually *did* live in Iowa and actually *was* a dental technician, had given him the low down on the job. "That and the crowns and bridges, orthodontic appliances too." He brought them to a stop. "And this is my room."

"Thank you for your help," she said, this time her smile genuine. "I owe you a drink."

He should beg off and keep his distance if he wanted to keep his cover, show Hollywood he could be more than just The Admiral, and finally get the respect he craved from a world that thought he'd only gotten where he was because of his parents. That's what he should do, but he didn't.

"Yes, you do," he said, unlocking his door with his free hand. "You know where to find me."

She looked down at her arm still in his, seemingly

surprised to find it there, and gently pulled back. "See you around."

And then she disappeared inside her room and Carter was left in the hall still trying to understand what in the hell had just happened and what he was going to do with a stranger's pants stuffed under his shirt.

TWO

Aubrey shut her cabin door behind her and let out the breath she'd been holding. Holy crap that had been close. If she'd been by herself there would have been no way she would have gotten away with it, giving the Boy Scout a gut had been a stroke of—

"Oh fuck." She let her head fall back against her door with a thunk. "You forgot to get Grace's pants back, you dumbass."

Now she was going to wait for Grace, Liv, Kendall, and Benjamin to vacate the hallway and then she'd have to go out there and knock on Carter's door. She cracked open her door; her friends were still out in the hall chatting away. Closing the door quick before they could spot her and interrogate her until the truth spilled out, she let out a frustrated groan.

Shit. Shit. Shitty McShittersons.

That's when she heard the knock. It wasn't coming from the other side of her door but farther inside the small cabin. There was a door connecting her room to the one next door. Bingo. The Boy Scout was her new favorite person for realizing it was there. She unlocked the door from her side and yanked it open.

"You. Are. Brilliant," she said. "I can't believe I forgot to get the pants."

He grinned, showing off a dimple in his right cheek deep enough for someone to get lost in. "No worries."

While she was still getting all lusty about a dimple, Carter pulled the hem of his shirt that had been tucked into the waistband of his shorts up. The move revealed a slice of abs as hard as his biceps and a very unusual wine-colored birthmark shaped like an A.

Aubrey's sorta-undercover-scoping-out gaze jerked to a stop on that birthmark. Suddenly her face was ten-thousand degrees and her palms were sweaty. She knew that A—not like personally or anything but she'd spent plenty staring at it on the screen in a dark theater because The Admiral movies were always about the fan service when it came to showcasing America's favorite superhero without his shirt on. And she knew from the many pics she'd posted on her Insta that the A birthmark wasn't movie magic, Carter Hayes had been born with it.

OH! MY! GOD!

He—Carter motherfucking Hayes—was still talking but she couldn't hear any of it over the roar of oh-my-fucking-God in her ears. How had she missed it? Sure, he'd bleached his usual dark hair (cutting it short enough that he could be mistaken for a Marine recruit), had on a dorky outfit, and was wearing a pair of glasses that her cousin in the military had called birth control glasses but still, she was a real fan. If any of her half a million Insta followers knew that she'd been fooled by this disguise she would never hear the end of it.

"Aubrey, are you okay?" He cocked his head to the side

and shot her a questioning look. "You kinda glazed over a little bit there."

"I'm fine." A slightly hysterical giggle started working its way up from her belly. "More than fine." She clamped her jaw shut in hopes of not letting the unhinged laughter out and said through her teeth, "Never been better."

She took the stack of pants he was holding out to her.

"So, I guess I'll be seeing you around?" he asked.

Clutching the pants to her chest, she nodded like a bobblehead glued to the dashboard of a car doing a hundred down a pothole-filled road. "Most definitely."

Okay, her ability to talk while freaking out was nowhere near the level she'd hoped it would be if this day ever happened, but who in their right mind would ever think they'd run into one of the biggest movie stars on the planet on a singles cruise. He wasn't even in the fancy suites. He didn't have a handler or people to, like, go fetch his coffee or anything. Maybe she was wrong. It wasn't like she'd gotten a great look at the birthmark. Maybe it was a common birthmark. Maybe there was a whole Facebook group dedicated to people who had birthmarks shaped like letters. Or maybe she was standing in front of Carter Hayes and her little brain had just broken in half. Yep. That definitely seemed like the most likely option.

"Don't worry, I won't use this door again." He held up his hands palms forward in the universal sign of I'm-not-a-serial-killer-intent-on-wearing-you-like-a-skin-suit. "I just noticed your friends were still out in the hall. Sorry for forgetting to give you the pants that you stole."

She nodded because her mouth had forgotten how to make word-sounding noises.

"Well, bye." Face screwed up in a look of half concern

and half WTF, Carter reached past her, grabbed the door-knob, and closed it between them.

A second later the click of the deadbolt being engaged on his side sounded.

That had gone about as well as eating one of the rock-hard bear claws she'd made back when she'd moved home to Salvation after her gran had first gotten sick. Her donuts were basically lethal weapons. Sorta like The Admiral's shield and trident. OMG. The Admiral!

Adrenaline making her hands shaky, she yanked her phone out of her crossbody purse and prayed for the little bars showing she still had signal.

"Yes!"

A few minutes later she had the perfect image—a GIF from Carter's latest movie showing him as The Admiral in disguise, strutting near the water, bonus points as it showed his amazing ass—and caption posted up on her Insta account.

Spotted on board? Still awaiting confirmation, but all signs point to The Admiral being in disguise on a singles cruise making its way down to the Bahamas. Tell me, what would you do if you spotted the very sexy Carter Hayes on your cruise? Thirsty me wants to know!

She closed the app and flopped down spread eagle on the bed, a little bit of guilt scratching at her conscious. Her anonymous super fan Insta had been her lifeline since she'd moved back to Salvation. Posting pics of The Admiral, chat-ting with fellow fans, and being generally a total dork about her totally-never-gonna-meet-him-so-it-doesn't-matter crush had been the one fun and silly thing she still did that reminded her of the fun person she used to be. Part stress relief, part hobby, it was a harmless escape from the three in the morning alarm waking her up in time to get the bakery open, the fear that the cough her gran hadn't been able to kick was something more serious the older woman refused to go to the doctor about, and the realization that everyone who'd told her that getting her degree in feminist history so she could write amazing non-fiction books sharing the real stories of women who'd done extraordinary things was a pipe dream was probably right. It was just for fun. It couldn't hurt anyone—especially not someone like Carter Hayes.

Still...she couldn't ignore that guilty-feeling. She opened up Insta on her phone to delete the post, but all of the signal bars were gone.

"Fucking A." Her groan was bone-deep and of the why-do-you-always-do-this variety.

Now she was going to have to go pay the GDP of a small country to get an hour of cruise ship internet so she could delete this post. And this is what she got for acting on impulse. Again. When would she ever learn to think before she acted and actually listen to her head and not just her gut?

"**W**ay to be a total creeper, Carter. What woman wouldn't freak out when a strange man knocked on the door connecting their rooms—all while they were trapped on a cruise ship together for the next seven days?" He rubbed his palm over the spiked-fuzz of his short hair that he still wasn't used to. "And please for the love of good beer and better women, do not start answering yourself."

Yeah, because he wasn't already treading that total weirdo line as it was. If she heard him mumbling to himself

—and answering—*that* would be the thing to really drive Aubrey into avoiding him.

"Whatever you say, buddy."

Carter had spent almost every day since he started noticing women around the most beautiful of them in the world. His parents were Hollywood royalty and that meant that everyone who was anyone, or who wanted to be, ended up at their champagne-drenched and cocaine-powered parties. Sometimes those folks took an extra interest in him. In the beginning, he'd thought it was genuine. He'd been an idiot. Of course, it wasn't. That wasn't the Hollywood way where every relationship was transactional and the best ones were those that either vaulted the other person from the B to the A list. That culture was so ingrained that everyone just assumed that the success he'd had on the screen was because of his parents. Now, Carter would be the first to admit that he had opportunities that others hadn't because of his parents, but no one placed the mantle of a billion-dollar movie franchise on a person because of who their parents are. Producers loved their money way too much for that.

Still, the need to prove himself as a man able to do the work and carry a movie without the help of his last name or the world's most talented special effects department was what lit a fire in him hot enough to burn down the Hollywood sign.

Right on cue, his phone rang.

"Carter, my man." His brother and agent, Byron, didn't sound the least bit winded even though odds were he was calling during the middle of his workout. The sicko trained hard and with the dedication of a body builder for the fun of it, not because the studio made him. "How are you and are you ready for me to send the rescue helicopter yet?

Carter glanced toward the sliding glass doors leading to his balcony. He could still see the New York skyscrapers in the distance. "We probably haven't even hit international waters."

"Did you get my gift?" his brother asked in one of his trademark oh-look-a-squirrel change of topics.

"I did. The condoms are a nice touch."

There was mountain of fruit, wine, cheese, and a box of condoms in a plastic wrapped basket that had been waiting in the middle of Carter's double bed when he'd opened his door. In addition to being his brother and agent, Byron was also the biggest troll alive so there was no doubt he'd included the condoms just to rub it in that Carter wouldn't be getting any during this cruise. The last thing he needed was getting his cover blown by getting a little too up close and personal with a rando or having someone spot his stupid birthmark.

"Hey, just because you're the uptight nerd version of Carter doesn't mean you have to stay celibate," Byron said as if he didn't know well and good that the very opposite was true. "My therapist says that it's important to express yourself and not bottle things up."

Carter rolled his eyes. "Isn't your unlicensed therapist also your weed dealer?"

"Hey man, it's L.A., everyone has to hustle."

"Speaking of hustling for work, is everything lined up for New York when I get back?"

Allyson Hernandez had all but triple-dog dared him into making this trip. It had happened during one of those awful Hollywood lunches at a restaurant almost no one could get reservations for. With several shelves full of awards for her movies, she didn't need Carter to get a table, however, being seen with him and even having it whispered that he might be attached to her next project could do wonders for getting financing for her next award contender. Meanwhile he wanted a shot—a real shot—at the lead part of a single father with a genius kid who had an attitude problem. So it was a transactional meeting, yes, but the tolerable kind where everyone involved was in on the real situation.

He'd made his case and Allyson had called over the waiter, asking the guy who she was sitting with. His answer? The Admiral. She called over a couple of others from the staff and got the same answer every time. He'd asked for one shot to prove he could disappear into a character, he'd do anything, all she had to do was name it. She'd told him about the cruise. He'd booked his spot right there at the table.

"I'm hurt that you'd doubt me on making that meeting with Allyson happen," Byron said with a huff. "We *are* brothers, you asshole."

"Exactly," he shot back. "That means I know you better than you know yourself."

And the truth of it being that his brother wasn't so thrilled with giving up guaranteed work for a chance at a maybe. Byron only believed in sure things.

"Such a dick. If only America knew what a pain in the ass The Admiral is." He paused, drawing out the moment as if they both didn't already know the answer. "Yes, it's all set up. You know she doesn't think you can carry it off. She says if you dock in New York and everyone on the boat hasn't made you, that she'll add another point of the box office if your audition is good enough for you to get the part."

"I don't want the points." How many times did he have to have this discussion with his numbers-obsessed brother? "I want the project. The story is amazing, it's—"

"Snore fest," Byron interrupted, his voice taking on the no-nonsense, cold-ass shark vibe that had earned him the reputation of being one of the scariest agents in the business. "Look, I love you, Carter, but I care about the points and believe me when you're too old to play The Admiral and get that kind of stupid money you will too. No one wants to end up like Mom and Dad."

Now that was the truth. It was amazing that when the parts dried up, the champagne ran out, and the cocaine dealer stopped delivering on credit how fast everyone fled. By the time their parents had to sell their house, the ranch in Wyoming no one ever visited, and all of the flotsam and jetsam from film sets that they'd collected over the years, there wasn't anyone left by their sides except for Carter and Byron. Their parents hadn't taken it well—that was one way to describe what happened, the tabloids had called it a Hollywood nightmare murder-suicide.

"I'm not crashing my career," Carter said, retreating from the edge of all those bad memories. "I'm diversifying. It's smart."

"I know, I know, just don't get too classy to think about the bottom line," Byron warned. "I know you love acting, but it's still business."

"That's why I have you." Byron was the one person in the world who he could trust to always have his back.

"And you're damn lucky for it." The unmistakable beep of the treadmill being turned off echoed through the line. "Have fun, nerd."

Carter chuckled. "You too, meathead."

"Always, man," his brother said, the booming, cocky confidence back in his voice. "It's hard to be as good looking as I am and not have fun."

Carter was still smiling when he hung up, but he

couldn't totally shake the oh-fuck feeling in his gut. This part mattered and he would do whatever it took to make this cruise a success and prove to Allyson that he could disappear into a part so well that no one saw even a hint The Admiral when they looked at him. Everything was riding on him staying under cover.

THREE

At the mandatory safety briefing Carter was sandwiched in line between a pair of guys who looked like they'd lifted so much their necks had permanently disappeared and the petite, just graduated from college-aged brunettes who had already hit the pool bar hard—all of whom ignored him as if he was just some regular guy in a stupid Hawaiian shirt. It was amazing. It had been years since he'd been ignored and he was kinda digging it.

His phone vibrated in his pocket and his gut sank. His brother wouldn't be texting unless there was bad news about the audition. Something had happened. He pulled out his phone and tapped the notification then took off his glasses so the face recognition would work.

BYRON: The gig is up.

Sliding his glasses back on, he looked around at the rest of the people out on the deck waiting for the safety briefing to start.

CARTER: What are you talking about?

BYRON: Your fav stalker Insta busted you on the cruise. That chick has fucking spies everywhere.

The Admiral Super Fan account had gone viral as soon as it had popped up. There were half a million subscribers and Carter's team was constantly battling it out about whether to find a way to shut it down or to just embrace the sorta-creepy but mostly-cheeky-and-funny vibe of it. For him, it was just one more reminder that for some people his life wasn't really his own so much as pre-packaged for their enjoyment. Mostly it was harmless. A few times—like after he'd come home to a fan swimming naked in his pool—it crossed the line. The ASF, as his team called it, wasn't one of the scary ones but they were a pain in the ass anyway. He couldn't take a trip to the gas station without it showing up on that feed. And now she knew he was here? Fuck him.

CARTER: No way.

A message alerting him of an incoming photo came in instead of a response from his brother. The downloading icon turned and turned and turned taking long enough that Carter had to check the urge to scream out a curse. He wasn't exactly known for his patience and this was fucking testing him.

Finally, the image loaded. It was a shot of him from the second The Admiral movie, an outtake scene where he'd been doing what one of his co-stars called the ass walk while still in costume for a scene in which The Admiral had been under-cover. The caption didn't name *which* ship he was on but there was enough information included—singles cruise, Bahamas— to have everyone on board doing double takes at likely suspects.

CARTER: Fuck

BYRON: Want me to send a rescue helicopter? The ship has a landing pad.

If only his brother was joking. He wasn't. Growing up like they did, they learned the importance—and the rarity—of actual loyalty.

CARTER: I'm not giving up. If that pain in my ass actually had a pic of me, she would have posted it. This could still happen. This could actually help.

BYRON: How's that?

CARTER: Shows I have skills.

It's one thing to hide in plain sight when no one was looking, but when someone was? That was even better.

BYRON: More like shows you have big dum-dum energy.

CARTER: I have one chance to get this part, to move beyond being The A. I'm not going down without a fight.

BYRON: Fine. I'll work my magic on this end. I'll get her to take it down, give you some more space.

CARTER: We've been trying to figure out who's behind the account for the past six months. You got a lead?

So far all they had was that the account was headed by a woman, because that's what she called herself, and that she had used every burner email and phone account known to man to set up her account. The whole thing was very clandestine and over the top.

BYRON: Twice you doubt me in one day. If I had actual feelings, I'd be hurt.

CARTER: Good thing we're safe.

BYRON: For now anyway.

Yeah. His brother may be a paranoid agent, but he wasn't wrong. Carter was only golden for as long as he could keep the Carter from Iowa cover in place. Stuffing his phone back in his pocket, he glanced around, trying to gauge if anyone was staring a little too hard at him, pretending to take a selfie while actually taking a pic of him, or getting a little too close—the basic annoyances of being a celebrity in public. Sure, he loved his fans. They were amazing and the reason why he got to do the job he loved. However, some days it would be nice to just be Carter the dude in the weird wiener-dogs-wearing-grass-skirts shirt.

"Oh my God, your shirt is just amazing," one of the women behind him said, her words coming out slow enough to let on how hard she was having to work to make herself not slur. "How do you make the dogs dance like that?"

Carter turned around while looking down at his shirt, trying to figure out what in the hell was going on. "Huh?"

"The sweetie little dachshunds." She giggled. "They move on your shirt." Then she looked up at him and lowered her oversized neon sunglasses. "Wait, you look familiar. Do we know each other?" She paused, screwing up her mouth and cocking her head to the side. "Have we banged?"

And yeah, this was not the kind of attention he needed to keep his cover. Still, he wasn't an actor for nothing. Figuring bad flirting would go over better than coldly shutting her down, he faked a nervous laugh. "No such luck on my part."

"You seem pretty sure about that, you don't even know where I'm from or what I do or my favorite movie—which is anything staring The Admiral because that ass. Oh my. I'd like to slap that and then give it a little bite." She made a little lion roar and used one hand to claw the air as her focus moved up his body until she got to his face. "I *do* know you." Raising herself up on her tiptoes, she planted one hand on his chest and leaned in close enough he might get drunk off her fumes. "Were you the guy in that video who did naked trampoline Zumba?"

Okay, that he had not been expecting. He shook his

head as he scanned the crowd, looking for something—anything—to distract his inebriated inquisitor. The woman's friend was flirting with both of the bulked up dudes. The people behind them were taking selfie after selfie. He turned and that's when he saw Aubrey walking in through the out door.

"Too bad." The woman let out a disappointed sigh. "That would have been something to recreate. Maybe we can anyway. And then—wait a minute." Her glassy eyes widened with recognition. "I know where I know you from, you're The A—"

"Aubrey!" He yelled, panic making his voice louder than he meant.

"The Aubrey?" The drunk girl hiccuped. "No. that doesn't sound right."

"My friend. Aubrey." He waved the pants thief next door over and when she got close enough, he grabbed her by the hand and yanked her over to his side, sending every silent message of "help me" he could with only his eyes and the squeeze of his hand. "We know each other."

Aubrey fell right into the game, pasting a huge smile on her face and nodding. "He went to college with my big brother. They both were in the same tabletop board game club." She gave the other woman an oh-my-God-right look when the other woman's expression turned skeptical. "Crazy right? We see each other for the first time since that epic two-week long game of Monopoly on a singles cruise."

"Monopoly?" The woman looked from Carter to Aubrey and back again as if she'd never heard of it before. "The kids' game?"

"It's fun for all ages," Aubrey deadpanned.

"That can't be right," the woman said with the kind of

stubborn confidence that only the mostly drunk had. "This guy he's got superhero arms. He wouldn't do that."

"There are all sorts of people who are in the tabletop board game world," Aubrey said, taking another step closer to Carter. "You wouldn't believe who's into it. Totally underground, fight club type of thing. No one can talk about it, but you seem cool so I'll tell you." Aubrey looked around as if she didn't want anyone to overhear. "Ryan Reynolds. Crazy for it."

"Really," the woman gasped.

"Totally." Aubrey nodded and lowered her voice. "But you didn't hear it from me."

The other woman mimed turning a key in a lock on her lips. Well, that was what she tried to do. What it actually ended up looking like was a woman about to jab herself in the eye with her thumb.

"If I could have your attention," said the cruise ship attendant at the front of their clump of people pulling everyone's attention her way. "The following information will only take a few minutes to hear but could save your good time."

A few people chuckled. Aubrey didn't. She looked a little green.

"Thanks for saving me," he said, realizing that he was still holding her hand.

He let go, his fingers tingling, and the idea—the solution to his undercover problem—hit him like all the best ones do, fully formed and just in the nick of time. "So you know how you owe me for the pants?"

She nodded, her gaze skittering away from him.

"I know just how you can pay me back."

Her eyes rounded.

Fuck. He was an asshole.

"No. Not that." Yeah, he was not trying to have sex with her, especially not to pressure her into it. Damn. It was a good thing he made his living speaking the words other people wrote for him. What he wouldn't do for a quick rewrite and a second take. "I put that the wrong way. I'll explain everything after we get out of here. Okay?"

Thank God getting out of here involved a drink with a teeny-tiny umbrella in it because Aubrey needed some aged in a barrel courage to make it through a face to face with Carter "The Admiral" Hayes without letting on that she knew who he was *and* that she had ratted him out to the world when he was obviously trying to stay on the down low. It really was a two rum punch with extra cherries guilty kind of moment. When would she learn to think first, act second, and to stop sabotaging herself?

You've only had your whole damn life to figure out that one.

They sat down in a pair of deck lounge chairs on the otherwise empty deck at the front of the ship (The bow? The hull? The lido deck? Like she had any idea). His feet were planted on the deck and he was turned so he faced her, his elbows propped up on his muscular thighs. Whew. It was hard enough not to drool when she was watching him up on the big screen. From less than a foot away there was no denying that the man needed his own forearm porn calendar. And an ass calendar. And a sexy dimples calendar. And—

Focus, Dean!

"So here's the deal." He took a long pull from his beer as

if he was gearing up to say something earth shattering. "My name's Carter but my last name isn't Van Steeple, it's Hayes."

In an effort not to flinch at what was coming next, probably something along the lines of "and you ruined my vacation by opening your damn mouth," she took another fortifying drink. That kept her from talking too, she just looked at him over the top of the hot pink drink umbrella with yellow flowers on it as she sucked down half her drink to keep from having to talk.

He cleared his throat, looked around, and then leaned in close. "Carter Hayes." He waited a beat as if expecting her to scream or freak out (too late). "The Admiral." Another pause. "Do you watch movies?"

Only every single one of his an embarrassing number of times.

She nodded but said nothing.

"Okay, you're much cooler about this than people usually are."

Well if by cool he meant utterly petrified into drinking almost an entire rum punch and praying for a giant shark to leap out of the ocean and onto the cruise ship's top deck to eat her in one bite, yeah, she was totally that.

"So, I'm trying not to let folks know who I am." He gestured toward his blond hair. "Dyed my hair, got these glasses, and ditched my normal wardrobe. However, it turns out I need some help making sure everyone knows me as Carter from Iowa."

And this was it, this was when she admitted that she knew who he was and had maybe sorta definitely blown his cover on Instagram. She'd explain that she was sorry and felt like total shit about it. Some of the tension in her shoulders lessened and she relaxed enough to power through the rum punch, which was mostly gone already.

Decision made, she opened her mouth and she fucked it up. Again.

"Why?" she asked.

"It's a long story, but let's just say that someone loves telling the world about me."

Fuuuuuuuuuuuuuuuuuuuuuck.

He was talking about her. Well, about her Insta page. The whole thing had started as a joke, a silly bit of stress relief. She'd never meant for it to have blown up like it had. All of the followers had just sort of happened, and well, he'd seemed so far away, so unreal, so unknowable, that the fact that her super fan page might impact him never even crossed her mind.

He was The Admiral for the love of all things super-powered.

That was then. Now? He was pretty damn real sitting across from her looking like she was the only person between success and failure.

Aubrey's gut clenched and she set her drink down on the little table between their deck chairs. She was such a bitch—also, she had to get downstairs and stand in the line that probably wrapped around the piano bar to sign up for internet so she could take down the post. Before that though, she needed to tell him the truth.

Wow. This is gonna be super fun in the chewing off a limb kind of way.

"If you're in agreement," he continued. "We can just use that perfect bullshit story you came up with for the drunk woman. I'll be your brother's friend from college. It's perfect. The board game thing was a nice touch. You're the only one on this ship who can help me. I can't risk telling anyone else who I am."

"I can understand that." Loose lips and all that.

"So are you game?" He gave her a hopeful smile that made his dimple appear. "A little backup help? I'll make it worth your time. Just tell me what you want."

The way he looked at her when he asked was a shiv to her guilty conscious. Her chest was tight, the rum punch in her stomach was swirling, and she couldn't stop jiggling her knee. Nerves? Guilt? Shame? How about all of the above.

However, if she deleted the post and helped him out on the cruise she could make up for the trouble she'd caused because she hadn't seen Carter as a person but as a famous dude who'd voluntarily relinquished his privacy. If she did him a solid, fixed things up, then what good would telling him the truth about her do? None. It would just complicate matters since the person he'd confessed his identity to was the last one he'd ever want to. Why shove that in his face?

Hey, Dean, stop projecting. You're the guilty party here.

It was true. And she was a chicken shit. She admitted it all in her head but...well...he'd never have to know the truth. Anyway, when he got off the ship without anyone being the wiser about who he was, he probably wouldn't even care.

Yeah, sure, Dean.

"I'll help," she said, her voice little more than a squeak. "And I don't want anything in return. Really."

"Thank you so much." He clinked his beer against her plastic cup. "You have no idea how much you're saving my ass. You're the best, Aubrey."

Oh yeah. Definitely. Without a doubt. She was the best shithead on this cruise.

FOUR

Plate loaded down with enough carbs for a marathon runner, Aubrey scooted in next to Grace at their table in the crowded buffet restaurant and took a sip of coffee. After a million dreams last night all involving Carter and her getting it on—which all ended with her telling him she had been the one who'd told the world he was on board and him denying her an orgasm as punishment—she'd woken up tired, unsatisfied, and desperate for caffeine.

Grace, however, had no fucks to give about any of that judging by the little divot of pissed-off-ness in the middle of her otherwise gorgeously unlined and fully moisturized forehead.

"I meant what I said yesterday," Grace said. "I want my pants back."

No one else said anything. Not a shocker, the pants stealing had been her idea. Liv had even tried—unenthusiastically—to talk her out of it. But the prank was too much fun for Aubrey to deny.

"No clue what you're talking about, and anyway, this is a

cruise, live a little." She took another sip of the world's best no frills coffee. "I'm sure whoever stole your pants will mail them back to your house as soon as we get to port in Orlando."

With a little snort of disbelief, Grace swiped Aubrey's mini chocolate croissant and—while maintaining unblinking eye contact—took a large bite. It reminded Aubrey of watching her gran's bakery cat give her the what-the-fuck-you-gonna-do-about-it glare as she pushed the canister of flour off the counter. Grace was out of pants and fucks apparently, which meant nothing but good things. Aubrey's lips twitched as the giggle built up. She smashed her lips together and tried to stay quiet. It wasn't gonna work. It never worked. Really, she should know better by now. Lucky for her, Grace was doing the silent chuckle, well, at least her eyes were because her hand was covering her mouth to keep the half-chewed croissant from flying out.

"You're the worst, Aubrey," Liv teased, shaking her head.

"And that's why you love me best of all," she shot back at her best friend from college.

Oh my God, the trouble they used to get in. Unlike her life now, everything then was all late nights, good times, and hot guys. Now she was early mornings, old guys who were regulars at the bakery, and cold brew coffee. But she was done thinking about that for the next six days. Instead, she was just going to bask in the awesome of getting to hang out with Kendall, Liv, Grace, and Benjamin as they enjoyed the eye candy, margaritas, and sunshine. Nothing was going to mess this up.

"There you are!" a man called out in a way-too-cheerful country bumpkin tone.

Shit.

She knew that voice. Awkwardly enough at the moment, she'd gotten off to that voice as he planned an arctic rescue mission in *The Admiral: Permafrost*, which she'd watched way too many times to ever admit out loud. Even worse, she'd probably get off to it again even though she now kinda knew him and he wasn't just the amazingly hot, chiseled guy who did that Salmon Ladder exercise shirtless and sweaty in every movie. Did that make her a bad person? Probably. She'd find a way to live with that.

"Aubrey, I've been looking everywhere for you." Carter slid into the booth next to her.

"You have?" she asked, trying to sound cool and normal and not like a woman who was picturing the naked sideview of *that ass*.

It was official. She really was the worst.

He leaned in close and lowered his voice. "Omaha. Three o'clock."

In a move that would have done The Admiral proud, she snuck a peek without making it obvious. A trio of women were clumped together, frozen in place as they stared at Carter. The other twenty billion people in the morning buffet getting their carbs and coffee on swerved around them like a school of fish dividing and coming back together around some mid-ocean impediment. It was wild.

"Did you put a spell on them?" she asked.

"No, they're just confused about who I am," he said, giving her an unmistakeable help-me-out-here plea with his blue eyes.

At the table, Benjamin looked like he was about start asking questions and Kendall had her tell-me-everything face on. Add that to the women who were starting to move closer to their table and it had all the potential to be a total disaster on the high seas.

"Oh for the last time, you do not look at all like The Admiral," she said, her voice loud enough to carry over to the port side or bow or whatever part of the ship they were farthest away from and most definitely carry to the ears of the women about to ID Carter. "Oh my God. The ego on this guy." She rolled her eyes at her friends before turning back to face Carter, her features set into a passive-aggressive and yet sympathetic mask. "No offense, but your nose is more bulbous at the end than his, your build not quite as perfect, and—bless your heart—my panties didn't immediately go up into flames when you walked by. You're cute and all but you're just the poor gal's Admiral not the real thing. There's no way you could get away with telling people you were Carter Hayes."

Watching out of the corner of her eye as doubt walloped the trio who were taking in every word out of her mouth, she smiled sweetly at her friends, who'd stopped eating and were giving Carter a closer perusal.

"So," she said, her brain spinning in an effort to get a kinda plausible story out fast enough to cut off any inquiry. "It turns out in a very seven-degrees-of-Kevin-Bacon way that we're connected. Can you believe that? He went to college with my older brother and they were in the same fraternity."

"Which one?" Benjamin asked, leaning forward so his forearms were on the table.

And that's all it took to turn the inside of her head into a total void. She had nothing. Oh God, she sucked at this whole subterfuge thing.

"Alpha Lamba," Carter let out a cough, holding up one finger in a non-verbal plea for a moment. "Duck."

Aubrey's eyes went wide. Duck? Really? Okay, she'd had a total brain coma but he'd gone with duck?

Too bad she didn't have any choice but to go with it. "It's an Iowa thing."

Kendall, Benjamin, Liv, and Grace didn't ask a follow up but she had no doubts they would later—and it would be epic.

Nice going, Aubrey Dean. You're world class.

"What was that?" she asked, leaning in close to Carter and keeping her voice as quiet as possible in the loud dining room.

"I froze." He shrugged. "My big nose must have gotten in the way of my brain."

It took just about everything she had not to lift her fist and shake it at the sky while screaming "men" at that moment.

"Don't be so sensitive," she said. "You've made the sexiest humans to have ever existed list, you'll live."

"Three times." He held up three fingers. "That's how many times I made the list."

"Really?" she whisper yelled. "That's what you're gonna focus on right now when your cover almost got blown straight out of the water?"

He snagged a mini-pastry off her plate, tore off a bite, and held it out as if to hand feed her. "Good thing I have you to save the day."

Then, he gave her a grin. It wasn't just any grin either, it was the one that one that showed off his dimples and made him look like a good guy who would do all the bad things—and her panties went up in flames as she accepted the bite.

Feeding Aubrey may have too much, but she was the kind of woman who inspired that kind of take-it-to-the-next-level reaction in him. He'd have to watch that. Just because he happened to have a thing for trouble-makers and wild women in general didn't mean he needed to get any closer to this one in particular. It didn't help that the move confirmed that her lips were as soft as he'd imagined last night. What could he say, all that rocking of the boat had given his dick ideas.

"So you went to school with Aubrey's brother, huh?" Benjamin asked, uh-huh-sure-buddy dripping from each syllable.

Yeah, that was not where this conversation needed to go. The less said about Carter the better. Time to redirect.

"That's right," Carter said with a nod before turning his attention to Grace, who was reaching down every other breath to tug at the hemline of her shorts. "Have your missing pants turned up?"

"No." Grace took a sip of juice. "It seems I won't see them again until I get home after the cruise."

"That's," he paused trying to come up with a response that wouldn't hint at his own involvement with the prank, "weird."

Kendall chuckled. "That's being friends with Aubrey."

"You have no proof it was me," Aubrey said, with a gasp that would have gotten her kicked out of any casting call.

"Just a long track record of shenanigans." Liv clinked her coffee mug against Aubrey's, a huge, conspiratorial smile on her face.

The byplay between the friends was straight out of a raucous comedy where friends who haven't seen each other in a while do something crazy when they finally see each other again. Kind of like booking a singles cruise. Hello, life imitating art.

"Oh really," he said, relaxing back against the seat and draping his arm over the back so his fingertips almost but not quite brushed Aubrey's shoulders. "She's a troublemaker?"

Liv leaned forward, planting her forearms on the table. "You wouldn't believe some of the things she got up to in college."

Oh, this should be good. "Try me."

A faint blush climbed up Aubrey's face until even the tip of her nose had a splotch of red on it. "You don't wanna hear these boring stories."

"Boring?" Benjamin said, his voice cracking in disbelief. "You're the reason why I started putting aside money for bail."

"That was only one time," Aubrey said as she sank back against the seat, the move bringing her shoulder into contact with his fingers.

The little buzz of awareness from something as small as that made him tense enough that he forgot to respond with a follow-up question that was desperately needed. Her friends, however, were already in storytelling mode and nothing was going to stop them.

"She went toe-to-toe with the local animal control agent who was trying to catch one of the cats that hung around our dorm," Grace said.

Everyone at the table—including Aubrey—started laughing at the shared memory.

"The charge was disturbing the peace," Kendall said between giggles. "AKA Aubrey has a big mouth and always jumps right into trouble with both feet without considering other options first."

"All of that is true," Aubrey said. "However, Wilfred Kitty didn't end up going to the kill shelter."

"And, of course there were the dates." Liv looked around at everyone else at the table as she took a bite of her breakfast. "What was that one guy's name?"

All of them groaned in unison.

"Chad," Aubrey said, her nose wrinkling with disgust.

Grace made a gagging noise. "That guy was the worst."

"He was convinced that Aubrey wanted to date him but she just didn't realize it yet," Benjamin said.

"Meanwhile our girl was already balancing at least three guys at a time," Kendall filled in. "There was no way she'd have time for a loser like Chad."

Now that he could picture. Aubrey definitely had the up-for-anything vibe. "No settling down for you?"

She shrugged. "Super serious relationships really aren't my thing."

"What is?" The question slipped out, violating his usual rule not to dig into people's private lives. With his own so completely under a paparazzi microscope, he'd learned to give others more space than the public allotted him.

If she was taken aback by the question, Aubrey didn't show it. She just tucked a few strands of her honey blonde hair behind an ear, revealing a line of piercings that went all the way up her earlobe.

"Sleeping in, chocolate covered cherries, and driving by pastures and saying 'look, horses' even if I'm by myself." She raised an eyebrow in challenge. "How about you?"

Fuck. He shouldn't respond to that tossed down gauntlet. But sitting this close to her in this half circle booth table, he couldn't help it. Sometimes when he was reading a script, he could tell by the end of the first scene if there was something special about it—a gut feeling that he couldn't explain or name. That feeling was buzzing through him as he sat in the middle of the crowded dining room and under the watchful gaze of Aubrey's friends. Fuck. If he didn't watch it, he'd forget the real point of being on this cruise—the one that had to do with the next stage of his career and not the next pair of legs he was getting between.

Still, instead of shutting it all down and deflecting back to her wild college days, he answered with the truth. "Watching the sunrise, fresh baked whole grain bread, and riding horses."

Across the table, Liv cleared her throat. "If only you two weren't eye-fucking each other over mini croissants and coffee we'd all be convinced you two aren't attracted to each other at all."

Startled, he flinched back, putting some space between him and Aubrey. Shit. How had they gotten that close together that his thigh was plastered against hers? That wasn't good. He had to keep his wits about him if he was going to make it through this cruise with his real identity under wraps.

Aubrey snorted and started fidgeting with the corner of her napkin. "He's friends with my brother and I'm not looking."

"So why are you on a singles cruise?" *And why do you keep asking questions, Hayes?*

She lifted her coffee mug and toasted the other people at their table. "To hang out with four of my favorite people in the world who I rarely get to see anymore." She turned back to him, her gaze going a little hazy when the move brought their legs back into contact. "Why are you here?"

"Get a feel for what life is like away from the soybean

fields and Buckeyes." That was the line he'd practiced repeatedly when he'd come up with this plan.

"So you're not looking for happily ever after?"

He shrugged. "My career is the only thing I'm concerned about having a happy ending."

And if he didn't stay at the top of his game, he wouldn't have one much longer. No place loved to spit out talent like Hollywood where there was always someone new waiting to take the lead. That's why this transition mattered so much. It was difference between a short stint as a superhero or a lifetime career. There was no in between.

"The workaholic and the rule breaker," Benjamin said before turning to face Kendall, Liv, and Grace. "Are we laying down odds yet for this?"

"That's a sucker bet," Liv said. "There's no way our girl has changed into the settled down, up early, in bed by ten life of domesticity."

"Well, I hate to suck all the joy out of y'all giving me shit," Aubrey said with a good-natured chuckle. "But Carter here has agreed to be my platonic plus one during the cruise." She snuggled in against him. "So I'll be nothing but good. Y'all will be the bad ones this time."

Liv lifted an eyebrow. "Now that really will be a first."

"Come on, ladies," Benjamin said, standing up. "We have a group massage scheduled followed by poolside piña coladas."

At the mention of massages and pools (translation: wearing only a towel or bikini), Carter's brain immediately took a sharp left turn to replay his Aubrey's naked fantasy from last night and getting up from the booth so she could slide out and join her friends became a little more fraught. Shit. Maybe he had been paying too much attention to work lately and not enough play. Having sex with someone under a false identity, though, wasn't something he was gonna do.

Of course, not everyone on board was in the dark about who he really was. He watched Aubrey as she strutted out of the dining room, his mind already spinning the possibilities that he most definitely shouldn't follow up on.

FIVE

There was nothing like giggles with her friends while drinking piña coladas by the pool to sand off the edges of the lingering reality of Aubrey's day-to-day life. Muscles loose, brain at ease, she walked out onto the balcony of her room to take in the breeze and the great wide swath of blue ocean that seemed to go on forever. A woman could get used to this life.

She sat down in the cushioned chair, extended her legs, and rested her feet on the railing. With opaque barriers that blocked off her balcony from the ones on either side of her, it was like having the ocean all to herself. Too high up to feel any splash from the water, it was still pretty indulgent in a way that getting up at three in the morning to make the donuts wasn't.

"I'll tell you one more thing," Carter said, his tone harsh with barely restrained fury as his voice carried over from his balcony to hers. "If you even think about crossing me, you'll regret it. I'll make sure of it. Remember what happened to Ricki? That was no accident."

The words were so cold, the intention so deadly, that

hearing them was like having ice water spilled down her spine. Aubrey straightened in her chair so fast her feet hit the balcony floor with a thunk. *Who in the hell is Ricki? What accident? Who is Carter threatening?*

"What I'll do to you will be worse than you living your pitifully boring life can even imagine," he said, a dangerous rumble bringing an extra level of ferociousness to his words. "Even your dentist won't be able to identify the body—*if* they ever find it. Got that?"

Holy shit. Whatever was going on, it wasn't good. Not even close. The sound of Carter's footsteps as he walked out onto his balcony sent her pulse spiking for all of the don't-get-murdered-for-overhearing reasons. Getting up as quietly as possible, she held her breath and reached for the door, praying it wouldn't make any noise so she could escape without notice.

"Glad you finally understand, asshole," he said, punctuating the statement with an unhinged laugh. "Fuck. That's not it."

Her palms sweaty, Aubrey pulled on the handle to slide the door open and nearly groaned out loud when it got stuck about two inches shy of her being able to squeeze through.

"Glad you finally understand, asshole," Carter said with an unnerving friendliness before letting out a frustrated huff. "Nah."

Giving it her all, Aubrey shoved the door.

"Glad you finally understand, asshole," he yelled as something hard slammed up against the barrier between their balconies.

Aubrey yelped and sprinted inside her room, yanking the door shut, locking it, and closing the curtains tight enough that it looked like dusk in her room. With her back pressed against the wall she tried to get her panicked breathing under control. What in the hell had just happened? What kind of nasty, scary shit was Carter into?

The knock on the door connecting their rooms was just barely louder than the blood rushing in her ears.

"Aubrey," Carter said through the door. "I'm sorry if I scared you. I was just running some lines."

She let it a breath because that actually made more sense than Carter being the kind of guy to put a hit on someone. He did collect spoons from every place he shot a movie, like some sort of grandpa—albeit one with washboard abs and an ass made for bouncing quarters off of. And yeah, she only knew that because of her internet stalking. Come on, she needed a happy place that didn't involve bear claws.

"Open up." He tapped on the door again. "I'll show you the script."

"Isn't that just what a serial killer would say?" Of course, that line lost some punch since she said it while walking across her stateroom to the connecting door.

When she opened it, he was standing on the other side in—Lord, have mercy—long hung swim trunks and hotness.

He held up a tablet with a script on it. "Henrique isn't a serial killer, he's a man pushed beyond any ability to realize how far he's gone. He's broken."

Kinda like her brain right now. All of the signals it was sending were of the can-I-lick-you-right-there variety. Fuck. She was such an asshole—a totally horny, oh my God those piña coladas had been a bad idea asshole. A very good bad idea.

Keep it together, Aubrey. You are more than just a sensitive clit and hormones.

"You wanna run lines with me?" Carter asked. "If you don't have better things to do."

"Yes." How she managed to get the single word out without squealing she had no idea.

"Exactly." He shifted and the muscle twitch in his jaw went into overdrive. "You're here with your friends. Go have fun. Don't let me interfere with your plans."

Plans? What pla—

Jesus, Aubrey. Get it together,

She shook her head trying her best to focus on the man and not just the abs. "I mean, I don't have any plans right now and running lines sounds fun."

"Here." He held out the tablet to her. "I have it memorized, you can use this."

She took the tablet, her fingers brushing his in the exchange, the small touch enough to make her catch her breath. *Damn, girl, you're on a singles cruise and you've got to go get laid before you throw yourself at this poor man.*

Not sure where to look without ogling him, she took the safe route and focused on the screen as she walked into his room. "What page?"

"Just pick one with the yellow highlights." Carter rolled his shoulders, stretched his neck from side to side, and changed his posture on a breath. "All of those are the scenes with the hit woman."

Watching out of the corner of her eye as he transformed before her, becoming somehow more hulking and brooding, she scrolled through the script. The pages flew across the screen before she stopped on the third section she saw with yellow highlight. Anna had to be the hit woman.

"So show me what you got," Aubrey read.

The muscle in Carter's jaw twitched and he rubbed the

back of his neck, the intensity lessening a few notches. "Maybe not that scene."

"Why not?" She double checked. Yep, definitely yellow highlight.

"There's kissing." He rubbed his palm across his buzzed-short hair. "I didn't ask you to put you in a weird position or make you uncomfortable. I wouldn't do that."

Alright, that was pretty standup of him and she didn't doubt him.

She shrugged. "We'll skip the kissing then." She glanced back down at the script, surprised she could still make sense of the words because all she could think about now was the kissing parts. "So show me what you got."

He let out a breath, changing the way he held himself, eyes going darker, harder. "What do you need?"

"You gotta nine?" She looked up at him, pausing a beat. "I hear it's your trademark."

Oh my God, that line. Sure, there was a script note that they were talking about a nine millimeter but that was not a subtle bit of dialogue there. A giggle at the ridiculousness bubbled up inside her, but she fought it off. Then, Carter took three steps closer, cutting the distance between them, a cocky smirk curling his mouth and doing things to her panties.

He winked. "That's what they say."

Anticipation, light and feathery, brushed across her skin as she looked down at the next line. "Let me see."

Guns, she reminded herself. They were talking about the weapons of their trade.

Carter strutted over, every step an invitation for trouble. "This is a mutual show and tell."

Aubrey gulped, digging deep to find the badass inside. "You go first."

He let out a soft chuckle. No, that didn't even do it justice, it was more of a touch in sound form, tactile and teasing in just the right ways.

Fuck. That wasn't fair. He shouldn't be this good at this because while her mind knew this was play, her body had other ideas—all of which centered around putting that mouth of his to use in ways that didn't involve talking.

He brushed a stray hair behind her ear, letting his fingers trace the curve of her ear as her nipples puckered against her bikini top.

"Darlin'," he said, his voice a rumble of heady promises. "I believe in letting the ladies finish before I do."

Yes, please. No wait. That wasn't the line. That was an actual thought, prayer, whatever. God, she needed to get laid. She glanced down, got her next line, and what would not be happening that.

"Don't you just have all the answers," she said, her voice breathy as she lifted her chin and moved forward so they were practically touching.

"Not all of them." He shifted, plucked the tablet from her hand, setting it down on the tiny desk in the room, and then pressed both of his hands to the wall on either side of her. Dipping his head lower so they were so close their mouths were practically touching he asked, "Who hired you?"

Did they pause here? Was she supposed to say "and they kiss?" His gaze dropped to her mouth as she tried to get her brain and her body to do what they were supposed to do when all she wanted was to follow the script. Then, before she realized what she was doing, her lips were brushing across Carter's. It was soft and chaste—in other words not nearly enough for what she wanted, needed right now. She wanted hard and demanding and take-me-right here against the wall.

Breaking the kiss at the realization, the reality of it all hit her. *Fuck.* They were running lines from a movie script, none of it had been real. He'd been worried about making *her* uncomfortable and she'd been the one to harass him. *Shit, I am so the asshole in this situation.*

"I shouldn't have done that. I got carried away," she said, pressing her back against the wall and wishing like hell that she could melt into it. "I'm sorry."

He kept his hands plastered to the wall but took the half step forward so their bodies were touching. "I'm not."

"That's not your next line." *Because that's a brilliant thing to say at the moment when you're about to explode from anticipation, Aubrey.*

He dipped his head lower, so close, but not nearly enough. "I know."

Oh hell, this was a bad idea—just the kind she couldn't follow up on in her small town without everyone knowing by dinner exactly what she'd done. But here on the high seas? She could be that carefree person she'd been back in college. God, she needed that if only for a few days.

"You want to go off script?" she asked as she trailed her fingertips over the hard planes and defined ridges of his bare chest.

His hands moved from the wall to her ass and he lifted her up, bringing her against him so that her core was against the hard length of him. "What do you think?"

Forget thinking. She was done with that until they docked back in New York. So she wrapped her legs around his waist and kissed him, nothing nice and sweet about this one. This was all want and craving and need for something more real than that.

Damn Aubrey felt good rubbing up against him, her full lips on his, her long fingers cupping his face, her smooth legs wrapped around him, and that sweet, hot pussy of hers against his dick. The moment she'd picked that scene he should have told her no way and stuck to it. He thought he'd be able to stand the temptation. What a fucking lucky idiot he was—something he should have realized the minute she'd open that connecting door. Just the sight of her in a light blue bikini top with her nipples poking against the thin material had his blood rushing south. Add the fish tattoo wrapping around her ribs that he immediately wanted to trace as well as the filmy blue wrap tied around her waist his fingers itched to untie and he knew the smart move would be to apologize and close the door between them.

But he hadn't.

"This really wasn't my plan," he said between trailing kisses across her shoulder, her skin still smelling of coconut sun screen and tasting of saltwater.

"Mine either." Her gaze not leaving his, she reached behind her back to the tie holding her bikini in place and tugged it loose. "Do you want to stop?"

There were a million things he wanted in the world, but with Aubrey in his arms none of them mattered. "Fuck no. I have too many ideas for what I'd like to do with you right now."

She pulled one of the strings tied into a bow behind her neck and her bikini top slipped off, falling to the floor. "More script reading?"

This was where the writers would put in a smartass line or a something catchy. His mouth was too busy with

Aubrey's tits for that. Adjusting his hold on her ass, he lifted her higher so he could take one of her hard nipples in his mouth, grazing his teeth over the hard nub and curling his tongue around it. Her grip tightened on his head as she let out a shaky moan. Switching sides, he teased her other nipple until it was wet with his attention and he blew on it, watching the stiff peak go diamond hard.

This was good but it wasn't enough. He wanted—needed—more.

Lowering his arms, he let her slide down him until they were face to face again. "Say the word and we stop immediately, no questions asked, but I'd like to take this to the bed. You good with that?"

"Depends." She snagged her bottom lip between her teeth and gave him a wink. "Are you gonna be naked?"

This woman. She was going to kill him and he'd die happy. He pivoted and lowered her to the bed before taking a few steps back, his hands going to the waistband of his swim trunks.

"As you wish." He shoved them down and made his way back to the bed, one hand curled around his cock as he jacked it slowly, looking down at her spread out on the bed.

Aubrey's gaze turned dark with lust as she watched him. Not that she wasn't busy herself. She made quick work of undoing the knot holding the wrap around her waist, revealing her blue bikini bottom held up by two very tempting bows on either hip.

The sight was the best and worst thing all at the same time because he was a selfish bastard. "Don't you dare take that off."

She paused, then lifted an eyebrow. "Why?"

"Because." Unable to go another minute without touching her, he spread her legs and ran his hands up her legs from her ankles to nearly the juncture of her strong thighs stopping just short of where he so desperately wanted to touch. "For as much as I want to have you naked, there is something to be said for anticipation."

She rolled her nipples between her fingers, pulling them taut. "You like to be teased?"

"No. I like to be the one taking it slow, making you want it more, hearing you plea for me to touch you..." unable to deny either of them any longer, he glided his thumb across the damp center of her bikini, "...right here, and then when you think you can't take it anymore, feeling you come so hard you squeeze my dick hard enough that I follow you over."

She let out a shaky breath and lifted her hips. "Take off my fucking bikini. Now."

"Someone's demanding." He toyed with the string, dragging the end of it across her upper thigh. "I don't know if I should do that."

Aubrey narrowed her eyes at him. "Carter. I'm dying here."

It wasn't even close to begging, but he was on the verge of pleading himself so he wasn't going to call her on it. Instead, he tugged the string until the bow was undone, repeating it on the other side and letting it fall to the bed.

"Fuck, darlin', you are so wet," he said as he traced along her glistening folds with the tip of his finger, watching her face for every change in expression, listening for each sharp intake of breath when he found the right spot.

And when he found that spot, the one that made her grip the sheets like she was afraid of falling off the face of the earth? That's when he dipped his head between her thighs and tasted her, taking his time as she lifted her hips and rocked her core against his mouth. Taking his time, he explored her, gauging her response to every lick, stroke, and touch, her responses making his dick harder. Scissoring his fingers inside her, he circled his tongue around her clit again and again.

"Don't stop," she said, her body going tense. "So close."

He had absolutely no plans of leaving her wanting. Having her sweetness on his lips and watching her as her pleasure built higher and higher was too good for that. The temptation to dial it back, take her off the edge of coming, was strong but denying her wasn't something he had in him. Especially not when she was making that soft moan between quiet yeses and pleas for just a little bit more. Instead, he gave her his all, everything was hers for the asking.

"Right there, Carter." Her staccato demand was a scream in whisper form. "Right. Fucking. There."

He pulsed his tongue against that spot, the one that made her yank at the sheets, until she came with a sharp cry, her back arching as she went over. Watching her come was the hottest thing he'd ever seen.

He couldn't wait to see it again.

Aubrey wasn't sure she still had bones anymore, every part of her had magically transformed into Jell-O. Okay, it hadn't been magic but Carter's tongue and fingers and the general oh-my-God goodness of an orgasm that had singed her all the way down to her toes. Refocusing her eyes was an effort of Herculean proportions but she managed just barely to do it and was rewarded with a view that would put the son of a God to shame.

Carter at the end of the bed, sitting back on his heels

still between her legs, his mouth wet with her satisfaction and the best kind of dangerous gleam in his blue eyes. Holy shit, if he could deliver on what he was promising with that look then her day was about to get even better. Could that even be possible? She was more than willing to roll the dice.

"Please tell me we aren't done," she said, propping herself up on her forearms to get a better look at him—and what a view it was.

The man might be undercover on the cruise but here in his room there was no hiding the body ripped enough to portray a superhero on the big screen. Spectacular? More like fucking mind boggling. She could wash the bakery's aprons on his eight pack—of course, she had other plans for him today.

Judging by the sexy smirk on his face that had his dimple sunk about a mile into his cheek, so did he. "Not even close to being done."

Liquid desire flowed through her as anticipation made her body tingle. "Condom?"

He leaned over and fished one out of the shaving kit on the desk next to the bed. "Got it covered."

Watching him roll the latex onto his hard dick was no hardship. There was just something about watching a guy handle himself that got to her, and made her think every dirty thought there was out there, plus some that probably hadn't been invented before.

As soon as he was done, he reached down and took her by the ankles and tugged until her ass was on the edge of the bed and he was between her splayed legs. "Fuck, you are delicious."

Then, he reached down and used his large hands to cup her ass and lift her up so only her shoulders were on the bed. What need was there for a sex pillow when there was someone with arm-porn worthy arms to hold her in place? Absolutely none. She was back to holding onto the sheets for dear life because he was about to rock her world and she was so here for it.

This wasn't for forever.

This was for fun.

Holding her with only one hand, he lined himself up with her opening and entered her slow, one thick inch at a time, filling her up completely. The rest of the world fell away at that moment. There was only her and Carter, the sounds of their bodies coming together and the tortured breaths as he fucked her slow and steady. The feel of him against her as he thrust forward into her and pulled back, leaving her wanting, had her begging for more in a voice she barely recognized as her own.

"You want more, darlin'?"

"Yes."

Carter withdrew completely, his big hands moving to her hips before he flipped her over so she was on her hands and knees, back arched, and ready. He sank into her, going deeper than before, so much so that her breath caught.

"Too much?"

"Give me a second." She released a deep breath, relaxed around him, and then pushed back against him, slow at first and then faster until she was practically slamming up against him.

"I could watch that ass of yours all damn day." He gave her a smack on the cheek with just the right amount of sting.

Looking over her shoulder she took in the man behind her, his eyes dark with desire, his jaw squared with intent. It was the hottest thing she'd ever seen. "Do that again."

He did. Once, twice more. Then he gripped her hips,

yanking her back, and they worked together, back and forth, thrust and retreat, deep and shallow, until they were both panting, their skin glistening with exertion. She was climbing, every nerve ending tuned into that place where their bodies were joined, an electric ball of fuck-yes building with each stroke. Reaching between her legs, she circled her clit, her fingertips brushing against his slick cock as he fucked her.

"That's it, darlin', squeeze my dick," he said, his voice thick with want. "So. Damn. Tight."

The sound of his rumbled order was all it took to send her to the breaking point. Fingers pressing against her clit, her orgasm rushed over her, sweeping her away on a wave of pleasure that nearly knocked her arms out from under her. Carter's harsh groan as he tightened his hold on her was all the warning she got before he rammed into her—hard, rough, and demanding—and then plunged into her one more time and came with enough force that she was probably going to have fingerprints on her hips.

Totally worth it.

"Let me go get rid of the condom," he said, his breath ragged, as he withdrew and walked to the bathroom.

Hello reality, so very not nice to see you again. "I should get back to my room."

"Why not stay?" he asked through the closed bathroom door.

"Do you think that's a good idea?" She was after all the woman who'd ratted him out to the world for being on this cruise. Guilt poked at her, made her chest tight. Post-coital confession time didn't seem the ideal time to fess up. Was it really so wrong to enjoy the afterglow for a few minutes?

"After what just happened?" Carter walked out of the bathroom, a Greek god in human form. "I think it's a very good idea for you to stay because I'm hoping you'll agree to do it again."

"You're a bad influence." *And you're a giant horny chicken, Aubrey Dean.*

He grinned at her and crossed over to the bed. "Without a doubt."

She should say no, gather her clothes, and walk bowlegged back to her room. That was the smart thing. But what no one ever tells you about orgasms is that sometimes they make a person very, very dumb. She rolled over and got under the covers. Her head barely had time to hit the pillow before the bed dipped under Carter's weight and he snuggled up big spoon style behind her, cocooning her in his warmth. After that, fighting sleep was a losing battle. When she woke up she'd explain what had happened, how she'd dimed him out before thinking better of it. He'd understand. God, she hoped so.

SIX

Cuddled up next to Carter, her head tucked into his shoulder, Aubrey refused to open her eyes despite the morning sun beating against her eyelids. That meant she most definitely was not going to get up, walk through the open connecting door into her room, and answer the damn phone that wouldn't stop ringing. She knew well and good who it was and she wasn't ready to retreat from the fantasy of being with Carter yet.

Did that make her selfish considering who she was, who he was, and what she'd done? Probably, but she was fixing her mess by being his cover story. That had to count for something.

Not nearly as much as honesty.

Aubrey squeezed her eyes shut and tried her best to block out her guilty conscience and the sound of the ringing that had started again. She just wanted to pretend for anther few minutes that the here and now was all there was.

"You should probably answer that before they send a search party," Carter said, his voice a rough rumble that was way too sexy for first thing in the morning.

He wasn't wrong. She let out a sigh and opened her eyes under protest—although the sight of a mussed up Carter wasn't a bad one. Really it was damn good. His hair was too short to be tousled but he managed to look just-woke-up sexy even with the pillowcase wrinkle across his cheek and especially because of the scruff covering his square jaw. Yep, that hadn't-shaved-in-a-few-days look really needed to make a comeback.

Focus, Aubrey Marie.

"Everyone was meeting up for breakfast and then deciding who wanted to go into Orlando and who wanted to stay onboard."

He rolled over onto his side, propping his head up with his hand and looking down at her, his gaze sliding over her like silk. "Which one are you doing?"

"Hadn't made up my mind." But was staying in bed an option because she was very much into that idea.

He hooked a finger under the sheet covering her from shoulders to toes and inched it down. "Stay on board with me."

"But I could go ride roller coasters." Never mind that the buzzy feeling in her stomach and the way every nerve was pulled taut had her already feeling as if she was approaching the crest of a loop-de-loop.

"Looking for thrills?" He tugged the sheet down farther.

She held her breath as it slid over her already hard nipples and they puckered even more in the cool air. Still, his gaze stayed on her face even as he kept drawing the sheet down lower and lower so slow it was as much a torment as a turn on until it sat low on her hips, the fact that she wasn't completely bared to him making her think about her impending nakedness even more.

"We can't stay in bed all day." Maybe just most of it with breaks for eating.

Carter slid his fingertips across her bare skin, just above the sheet. "Why not?"

Her stomach growled. Correction, it didn't make one of those cute little roars. It was more like the sound of an underwater violin being played a sea witch, all twangy high notes. Embarrassing? Only utterly and completely. Carter's hand stilled but his lips twitched as he tried to hold back a laugh. Then it happened again. She sounded pretty much exactly like one of her gran's dogs before they went outside and ate half a yard's worth of grass.

"Pretty soon that's going to get even worse," she said because it wasn't like she could blame the weird sound on anyone else in the room. "I need to refuel."

He gave her a quick kiss and got out of bed, which gave her the very best view of his ass. Shit. She was going straight to creeper perv hell but not staring wasn't an option—especially not when he turned around, hands on his lean hips, and gave her the full Monty. Thinking became optional.

"How long do we have before your friends send out a search party?" he asked, no doubt more than a little aware of how good he looked and exactly what he was doing to her.

The phone in her room started ringing again. God love her friends but she was going to have to kill each and every one of them. "Not long enough, but we can make up for that after breakfast."

"I'm coming?"

"Yeah," she said, tossing the sheet the rest of the way off and getting out of bed. "This is your official invite. You can work on your Iowa accent."

"Midwesterners don't have an accent," he scoffed.

She started at him in Southern. "Bless your heart."

Two incredible—and sadly separate—showers and about twenty minutes later, and they were walking into the dining room headed straight for the big round booth Liv, Kendall, Benjamin, and Grace seemed to have claimed. It wasn't until they were tableside getting the full top knot to toes perusal that it hit Aubrey just how obvious it was what had happened between her and Carter. Both of them still had damp hair, he definitely had a tiny bite mark at the base of his throat, and if anyone looked at the hem of her shorts they'd never miss the beard burn on the inside of her thigh.

Liv took one look and them both and said, "Imagine you two rolling in late together."

"Our rooms are right next to each other." The lie came out sounding exactly like what it was.

Benjamin covered his chuckle with the absolute worst impression of a sudden coughing fit ever as they all got up from the table.

"Wait, are y'all leaving already?" she asked, noticing that only the crumbs were left on everyone's plates and their coffee mugs were all empty.

"We've been here long enough for firsts and seconds," Grace said, shooting them a knowing grin. "Looks like it's just the two of you."

And they left. After all that calling and everything else, they took one look at her in her obviously just-been-fucked glory and walked away, leaving her alone with Carter. They really were the best friends ever—that was if she could figure out what to do now because the guilt eating away at her stomach lining for making that Insta post made acting like this was anything close to a normal situation impossible.

As soon as Aubrey's friends left, everything turned weird and Carter couldn't figure out why. She barely made eye contact and had left enough space for several of her friends to sit between them if they came back. Something had gone wrong between getting to the dining room and her friends leaving. What? He had no fucking clue.

So as he took another bite of his omelet, he fell back on one of the exercises he'd learned in acting class. Scanning the room, he spotted a woman in a neon T-shirt with what had to be a Bloody Mary winding her way across the dining room.

"See the lady in the lime green shirt?" He nodded his chin toward the woman. "You might think it's a bit early for a drink, but that's not an ordinary Bloody Mary. It's filled with a topical poison and she's about to spill it on the guy with the pineapple shirt and he won't realize he's going to die until it's too late."

"What are you tal—" Aubrey stopped mid bite, her eyes going wide and a then her mouth curved into a huge smile as she focused her attention on the man in the fruit shirt. "I see. But what neon shirt doesn't realize is that the old lady isn't pineapple man's mother, she's his bodyguard."

He kept his face turned toward the women in neon but was really watching Aubrey out of his peripheral. "She's obviously with the badass grannies motorcycle gang."

Aubrey nodded, her posture relaxing as she got into the game. "They *are* fearsome."

"Granny and pineapple man are on the lam." He moved over on the bench seat of the semi-circular booth until they were hip to hip. "They offed neon shirt's sugar daddy after a round of underground cockroach racing."

She snagged a slice of bacon from his plate and used it to point at the woman in the neon shirt as she stood in line at the waffle station behind pineapple man. "So it's revenge."

"Nope, a double cross." He grabbed his bacon back and bit it in half, giving her the remainder. "They were supposed to wait until he'd made neon shirt his sole beneficiary. They jumped the gun. Now they're all out ten million dollars."

Aubrey shook her head and let out a tsk-tsk. "Sometimes murder doesn't pay."

"That's definitely the title of the true crime book written about it—*Sometimes Murder Doesn't Pay*."

She ate the bacon. "Which, of course, becomes an international best seller inspiring its own secret cosplay groups of people who reenact that fateful day when pineapple man was poisoned."

"So the question is..." He pivoted in his seat, dropping his voice to a dramatic whisper. "What if we somehow entered a time warp and these are not the actual participants but the cosplay version?"

She threw back her head and let out a laugh. "Oh that was a great twist. I'd buy a ticket to that movie."

Carter sank back against the seat, his arm stretched out along the back of the booth behind her close enough that he wound the end of her soft blonde hair around his fingers. Aubrey leaned into his side, her hand dropping to his thigh not nearly as high on it as he would have preferred but this was the ship's main dining room and drawing attention for getting a public hand job probably wasn't the best idea. Of course, being around Aubrey made all sorts of bad ideas sound good. She had that effect on him.

"You got plans for later?" Because he definitely had plans for her and all of them involved getting naked.

She looked up at him with that same ornery twinkle in her eyes she'd had when he'd caught her rooting around Grace's suitcase for her pants. "Are you up for having your ass handed to you in shuffleboard?"

Little known fact. He brought a foosball table with him to every movie set and held a tournament open to crew and actors alike for a championship. It had come down to him and the cinematographer on the last Admiral location. He'd won after a quadruple overtime. Competitive? Him? Fuck yes. He'd never played shuffleboard a day in his life but that didn't mean he wouldn't win.

"You don't think I can hang?"

Aubrey lifted an eyebrow, nothing but challenge in her as she slid out of the booth and stared back at him, one hip cocked out in defiance. "I am the Hog Wild shuffleboard champion three years running."

"Oh we've got a badass here, huh?" He followed her out of the booth. "Thinking of joining the granny gang when you're older?"

"Joining?" She snorted. "I'm going to run it."

And three games of shuffleboard later, he was pretty sure she'd run the gang like she ran his ass on the painted deck. He hadn't just lost, he'd been destroyed. Now, deep into the fifth game he wasn't playing to win anymore, he was using his ineptitude as an excuse to be close to Aubrey.

Was it pathetic of him to have sweet talked her into teaching him how to play so that she'd stand behind him and wrap her arms around him to teach him proper form? Most definitely. He was okay with that.

"How did you learn to do this?" He took a step back so

he could get the amazing full view of her in those shorts as she lined up her shot.

Creeper? Him? When it came to Aubrey it seemed so.

"There's not exactly a whole lot to do in Salvation." She did this shimmy thing with her hips and slid her puck forward with just enough speed to bang into his and knock it off the board. "It was either go play shuffleboard at Hog Wild, our local honky tonk, or traipse out into the woods to help Ruby Sue with her moonshine operation. I went with the one that wouldn't end with me in jail."

"Is that where Ruby Sue is?" he asked as he walked over to the wall near a support divider.

It was a spot he'd already noticed was shielded from the view of people walking the other way on the deck and the ping pong table around the corner. He put his shuffleboard stick into the holder attached to the wall and sat down on the single lounge chair, daring her without saying a word to come over.

"Are you kidding?" Aubrey laughed and strutted her way to him. "She's got to be in her seventies at least and is the only one who knows the secret ingredient in her pecan pie recipe so no one else could make it if she got locked up. I pity the sheriff if he ever tried to lock up Ruby Sue." She put her stick next to his and sat down on the chair between his legs, leaning back against his chest. "The town of Salvation would turn on him before the single light on Main Street turned from green to red."

He wrapped his arms around her, holding her close as they both looked out onto the horizon. "What's your life like when you're not kicking ass at shuffleboard?"

"Not the way I expected it to be that's for sure," she said with a chuckle.

Aubrey might be trying to keep it light but there was no

missing the tension stringing her tight. For the first time since they'd met it felt like he was getting to see more of the person she was rather than just the image she presented to the world. If he was someone else he may not have realized, but there was no one more equipped to understand perception versus reality than a guy who'd spent the past decade in Hollywood. Life had taught him that there were always layers.

"I went back to help my gran out at her bakery thinking that I could sell some donuts and write on the side," she continued. "That was my plan anyway. But then Gran had a stroke. She recovered fully—thank God—but she can't take care of things like before and I'm all she has left so I'm not going to leave her."

He could picture that. Watching her interact with her friends—even when she was stealing one of their pants—showed just how much they all cared about each other.

"What do you want to write?" he asked, genuinely curious about what else she was hiding behind all that impulsive extrovert exterior.

"Narrative non-fiction about people like Andrée Borrel who was the first female paratrooper who was recruited to parachute into occupied France to train the resistance, or Gertrude Benham who circumnavigated the globe seven times before she died in 1938." The words came out in a rush of excitement, as if they'd been building inside her for a lifetime, leaving a heavy silence after they were all said as if she needed a minute to box all those hopes and dreams back up. "Instead, I'm up at o'dark hundred making donuts and running the bakery. It's hard to travel for research if you have to fill the Long Johns or refill the coffees of the old men in town who spend their mornings gossiping over crullers before handling the accounts, putting in the supply orders, and everything else involved in running a business."

"So you're doing what you need to do but not what you want. I can understand that."

"No offense," she said, sitting up and twisting around at the waist to give him a look of disbelief. "But are you serious? You know what that's like, Mr. Movie Star?"

Not surprised by her reaction, he shrugged. "I want more than to be The Admiral." He paused, waiting for the lightning strike from the fates or the super fan with the IG to pop around the corner, phone at the ready to snap video of his confession. He'd never said that out loud to anyone except his brother. He hadn't planned on saying it out loud to Aubrey. It just sort of happened. It seemed confessions to virtual strangers who a person never saw again wasn't just a thing that happened in the movies. "That's not to say I don't appreciate everything that's happened. I do. I know a lot of people don't get the chances that I have. Still, I feel hemmed in sometimes or like I betrayed the person who I was going to be."

"That I feel." Aubrey relaxed back against him, letting out a long sigh. "I love my gran but I miss that person I was in college. She was fun and had all sorts of plans and dreams."

"Is that what this week is about for you, getting some of that back?"

"At least for a little while, yeah I guess it is." She sat up, her ornery sparkle glinting again in her eyes. "Speaking of which, how about we play one last time and loser buys ice cream?"

The quick conversation change nearly gave him whiplash but he understood. There was giving someone a peek at the soft underbelly and then there was throwing everything wide and letting someone really take a long eye full. He wasn't into that either.

"I feel like I've been hustled," he teased. "Don't think it went unnoticed that you really were telling the truth about being a champion shuffleboard player. I thought it was hyperbole. Are you keeping any other secrets that I should know about?"

Her cheeks turned pink and she hurried off the chair, all but skipping a few steps away in her rush. "Forget the game, let's just go grab ice cream. My treat."

Seriously, he was going to need to get a neck brace if she kept switching things around so quickly. Not that there was any question of him not going with it. Ice cream and Aubrey were a pretty damn good combination.

"You footing the bill would help my damaged male ego," he said, playing it up with a melodramatic sigh that would have gotten him fired from a regional theater group.

"Heaven forbid that take a beating." She rolled her eyes, not buying it for an instant. "Come on, there are waffle cones with our names on them."

He hadn't planned to hold her hand as they walked to the ice cream stand near the pool, but it just came naturally —sort of like how he'd trusted Aubrey with the truth about his career. If anyone got ahold of that story it could ruin any goodwill the public had for him, but he could trust her. He just knew it in his gut the same way he knew within the first few pages of a script if it was a winner. Aubrey wouldn't do him wrong.

SEVEN

Belly filled with ice cream and the taste of hot fudge still on her tongue, Aubrey didn't understand the sudden on-set shyness as she stood next to Carter in front of her stateroom door.

"Thanks for the ice cream." He rubbed his palm across the back of his head hard enough that it would have messed up his hair if it had been even half an inch longer. "I haven't had a double scoop forever."

"They keep the ice cream freezer under lock and key?" she asked, teasing.

"I can't complain too hard. I have it a lot easier than the women in Hollywood do. Still, all it takes is a couple of unflattering pictures posted on some fan Instagram account to make casting directors thing I may be losing my appeal."

Maybe like her Admiral thirst trap account? Guilt sent her sugar rush crashing as she glanced down at the gaudy hall carpet and away from the man she'd been ogling in public but had never imagined would ever appear in her life. Lusting after him had been like dreaming in detail about how she'd spend every penny of her Lotto winnings even though she never bought a ticket.

"I'm sorry," she said.

He crossed his arms and leaned one shoulder against this door. "What for?"

She wrapped her arms around her middle and let out a deep breath. "I might have been one of those people who posted pics." Not a lie but definitely not the whole truth. Damn. Why was this so hard?

Lifting an eyebrow, he gave her a cocky grin. "Might have, huh?"

Despite knowing she should keep this moment serious, she giggled. What was it about Carter that made her feel like that person she'd been in college? The one who did dumb things occasionally but things always worked out. It was like being around him made her forget the clock-in, clock-out boring sameness her life had become.

"So," he went on, pretending to be shocked, "all this flirty banter hasn't been only because you're interested in my super-hot, big brain?"

Falling into old habits, she went with the moment, sliding into the safety of old, sassy, always up to something Aubrey. "Your butt might be kinda nice."

"Kind of?" He let out an exaggerated gasp, really going all in on the biting Hollywood egomaniac thing. "You know I was one of People's Sexiest People Alive."

"But you weren't named *the* sexiest."

He chuckled. "Only the best for you, huh?"

"Yes." She nodded, playing her part. "I have very discriminating tastes when it comes to Hollywood hotties pretending to be a local yokel from Iowa."

"I understand." He grinned at her as he opened his door. "See you at dinner?"

"You bet."

She was still doing that goofy-smile-happy-sigh thing when the closed the door and then ducked into the bathroom to grab her dress for dinner. She'd hung it up before her shower in hopes the lazy-person's iron would get rid of the wrinkles that her just-stuff-it-in-the-suitcase-and-go packing style had created. Survey said—she held up the blue dress with spaghetti straps and a suck-in-your-gut-and-pray zipper—yeah, close enough.

One tight-space strip down later and she was in the dress, zipper half down but a woman needed more room than was allotted in a teeny-tiny ship's bathroom to do the reach-behind-grow-her-arms-three-inches-to-reach-it-all maneuvers necessary to finish the job.

Her phone on the desk caught her eye as she walked back out into her room. Since they departed, it had been a glorified alarm clock radio but they were docked in Orlando, which meant she had signal. Finally! She could delete the post that started it all. Heart doing the thunka-thunka rhumba at twice the normal speed, Aubrey tossed her old clothes on the bed, picked up her phone, clicked on Insta, and instantly regretted the double scoop of hot fudge.

The notifications had gone wild. There were so many comments on her could-Carter-Hayes-be-on-a-singles-cruise post that it was like they'd made their own little comment babies. People were describing in all sorts of way too much detail exactly what they'd do if they discovered Carter was on their cruise. Wow. Folks were creative. She would have just been thinking bang him, but some of the commenters had gotten way more creative about the how, the when, the where, and the what exactly. If it wasn't sorta weird because she knew him, she would have been impressed by their creativity. But she did. He wasn't just The Admiral anymore. He was Carter.

Not needing any time to second guess herself, she hit delete on the post. Too late? Most definitely. But it was all she could do without a time machine. Too bad that didn't make the situation any better.

She dropped her phone on the bed and groaned. "You are such an asshole, Aubrey Dean."

"Did you poison my ice cream?" Carter asked.

She did a surprised squeak whirl around thing, her palm pressed to her chest above her wildly beating heart. He stood in the door that, like a dork, she'd forgotten they'd left open. He was in slacks and a button-up shirt that hung open, his to-die-for abs on display, but that's what she noticed last. The first? The way all of the jittery, anxiousness twisting her up inside melted away at the sight of him.

Oh this was bad. This was so bad. This wasn't just hanging out for a cover story, not for her anymore, this was so much, "Worse."

"Did you poison *all* the ice cream?" he asked.

This was when she told him. She just let it all hang out there, knowing he'd realize who she really was and that would be that. He'd close the connecting door and never talk to her again. Well, it was amazing while it lasted. And not because he was Carter Hayes, movie star and all-around eye candy. It was because he was Carter Hayes, the guy *not* from Iowa who made her laugh and gave her the maybe-this-could-be-more feelings.

Straightening her shoulders, she looked him square in the eyes and— "I can't zip up my dress."

No. That was not the words that were supposed to come out. They. Were. Not.

"I can help with that," he said, walking into her room. "Turn around."

God help her, she did. She was weak. And he was— well, he had that rough edge to his voice that did things to her. His hands went to her hair first, twisting it around his hand into a tight ponytail that he tugged with just the right amount of force to make her nipples stiffen and her breath catch. She closed her eyes and took a moment of oh-my-fucking-God before he let go and her hair fell over one shoulder. He walked his fingertips down the back of her neck, following her spine lower, his touch a teasing promise of what could be. Temptation didn't even begin to cover it. She had to get herself under control. She had to, *oh*—

He tugged at her zipper, lowering it. "This thing isn't working right." He dipped his head, brushing his lips across the nape of her neck. "I guess the only choice is to take it all the way down."

Desire, hot and demanding, licked at her skin as the sound of the zipper and her own pulse filled her ears. "Carter."

"I promise to buy you dinner later," he said, his breath hot on her skin as he slipped his hands inside the opening of her fully unzipped dress that hung loosely by the straps.

"You don't have to it's—"

"It should be clear by now," he nudged her dress down, letting it slip down her body to the floor, "that I want to." He cupped her breasts, taking her nipples and rolling them until they were hard, stiff peaks. "If you'd don't, tell me now."

It wasn't that. Oh God, it wasn't that. She opened her mouth, fighting against the want and the need telling her to shut the fuck up, but before she could form a half coherent thought, he slid his fingers under the band of her panties and she was lost to the heat and the ecstasy and the hope that somehow this would all work out.

———

This wasn't the first time that someone got nervous around him. They were cool right up until it hit them that he was The Admiral. Then, there was a shyness, a hesitancy that hadn't been there before. It was just one more weird thing about making his living pretending to be someone else—sometimes people bought into it much harder than he did. Usually it was just a bummer, but with Audrey? He wasn't willing to just accept it and walk away per standard operating procedure. He wanted—needed—her to see him as Carter the man, not Carter The Admiral. If he took the time, maybe he'd figure out why that was his new reality, but trying to make logical deductions was impossible while his fingers were wet with her desire and she was making that needy sigh each time he slow circled her clit.

"Does that feel good?" he asked, dipping two fingers inside her, fucking her in a soft slow rhythm that only made both of them want more.

Her answer was to press back against him, rubbing her ass against his cock and making him regret more than anything else in the world that he had on so many clothes. *Fuck*. He wasn't just hard, he ached and his balls were pulled up tight against him

"Aubrey." God, he loved saying her name. "You have to say it." He withdrew his fingers, pulled free of her ridiculously skimpy lace panties, took half a step back, and severed their physical connection though he swore he could still feel every inch of her. "I need to hear that you want this as much as I do."

Did he mean the sex? Did he mean something more? Did he mean everything and anything? Yes. He couldn't explain it and now sure as hell wasn't the time to dive into it.

She stilled and for a moment he thought this was it, she was done. Then, she whirled around—hands on those glorious full, rounded hips of hers—and looked up at him. Her pink panties were damp with her desire, the darker color matching the rose of her hard nipples. Damn. He could look at her all day—another day, today he wanted to sink balls deep in her and fuck her until she came so tight around his dick he saw the universe.

"Do I want you?" she asked, trailing a finger across his chest as she looked up at him, bold as brass and unapologetic.

The woman didn't have a coy or double-dealing bone in her body. Coming from where he did, where everyone was using everyone else and image was everything, her ballsy attitude was almost as addictive as she was.

"That's what I need to know." He shrugged off his shirt. "Do you want me?"

"Let's get these off so I can show you." She went straight for his pants, her fingers aiming for the button on his pants, a daring smirk on her pale pink lips as if she couldn't wait to see just how far she could take this. "Take off your pants so I can show you."

He took her wrists in one hand, lifting them above her head and backing her up against the wall. "That's not how this is gonna work."

She made a tsk-tsk sound. "You're keeping your pants on?"

"No." He kissed her hard and brief, barely giving either of them even a taste of what they wanted. "*I'm* going to show *you*."

"Are we having a fight?"

Immediately, he let go of her and took a step back, his gut twisting. *Fuck.* That was not what he was going for. He didn't want her to feel pressured. *Way to go, Hayes. This is why you need writers.*

Aubrey shook her head, letting out a soft giggle, then said in a stage whisper, "If you say yes that means we get to make up."

Make up? What did they have to make up for— Realization was like a lightbulb in the darkness. Oh yes. He was here for this little game.

"In that case, this is a huge," he flicked open his top button, "knock down," he lowered his zipper, "drag out fight."

She reached out, repeating his move and wrapping her fingers around his wrists before he could shove his pants down. "So angry sex?"

"Fuck yes."

One side of her mouth curled up and shoved his pants down over his hips so they and his boxers fell to the ground. "Just so you know, I hate these panties."

"Good because they're not going to be salvageable after this." He hooked a finger in them and the thin strap of lace snapped along with the last of his control.

In the next heartbeat, he had her pressed up against the wall, his hand encircling her wrists and holding her arms above her head, as he brought his mouth down on hers. It was like touching a match to the fuse of a firecracker, exhilarating and with enough sizzle of danger to make it more than a little fun.

Using his free hand, he traced a line down her side as slow and soft as their kiss was hard and fast. Damn, it was killing him not to rush this but he knew the payoff would be even better if he lingered, let the need build while he kissed his way down from the sensitive spot below her earlobe to the delicate place where her shoulders met her neck. While she begged for more, he trailed the back of his knuckles over the soft fullness of the side of her tits. Following the dip of her waist, he had to force himself not to speed up as he kissed lower, sucking her peaked nipple into his mouth, grazing the hard nub with his teeth. He was balancing so precariously on the verge of giving in to the urge to take her and make her his that when she let out a lusty moan as he traced the outward curve of her hips, his balls tightened and any idea that there was a world out there beyond them disappeared. By the time he finally circled her clit and slid two fingers inside her, she was so sweet and slick that it took all he had not to drop to his knees and taste his fill until her thighs were quaking on either side of his face as she came.

"You dare tease me any longer," she said, her voice husky with want. "And I'm going to tell everyone that you stole Grace's pants."

He shrugged, playing along. "Guess I'll have to live with that."

"I don't think so," she said, curling one of her legs around his as she shoved him and sent him flying.

He landed on his back on the bed with Aubrey straddling his hips. Hands on her hips, he was ready to flip her when she leaned forward so her tits dangled over his face and he forgot how to breath, think, move, do a damn thing beyond want. Somewhere in the background he heard a drawer open and shut before she leaned back, a wicked grin on her face and a condom in her hand.

"I'm done waiting," she said as she tore opened the condom.

"Yes, ma'am."

She unrolled the condom over his cock and lowered herself down on him. Watching her as she put her palms against his chest for balance and bit down on her kiss-swollen bottom lip as she took him in, had him doing math in his head to keep from coming before they'd even started. Then she started moving and he knew it was nearly game over. Tits moving as she undulated against him, he gripped her hips, bringing her harder against him on each downward stroke. Lifting his hips, he met her with ever plunge and retreat, letting her take what she needed, loving getting to see her face as she lost herself in the moment. Fuck, she was pretty with hot fudge on the tip of her nose, but like this she was absolutely gorgeous. And when she sped up, tightening around him as her nails dug into his chest, he wasn't ready for all of it to end but he didn't have the strength not to follow her over the edge as she came. His orgasm sling-shotted from the base of his spine to his toes and back up again, leaving him empty of everything except the realization that there was no way he wouldn't be seeing Aubrey again after the cruise was over.

Draped across his chest, her body loose and limp, she kissed his shoulder. "We should fight more often."

He chuckled, his eyes already too heavy to keep open, "I'll try to make that happen."

And then he feel asleep, sated for the moment, if not forever. Would he ever be when it came to Aubrey Dean?

EIGHT

Baseball hat on and pulled low, ridiculous swim trunks covered in hot pink pineapples in play, and the hottest woman on the ship sitting next to him getting all the sidelong glances from the other passengers on the boat taking them from the ship to the cruise's private island, Carter was feeling more than a little cocky about how his disguise was working out. No one gave two shits about him. It had been more than a decade since that had happened, right about the time that the first Admiral movie came out. The worst was when he got called out in mid-chew at dinner. He loved his fans for sure, but sometimes he just wanted to eat a cheeseburger with onions and not read a snarky post later about how he had the worst breath in Hollywood.

"Are you sure you want to take this risk?" Audrey asked as she looked around at the other passengers packed in around them, obviously nervous enough about him being exposed for both of them. "People do stay on the ship during these excursions. It wouldn't be that weird."

"True." He scooted closer to her on the bench seat until

they touched from knee to hips to his hand around her shoulders as he toyed with the ends of her hair. Usually he wasn't much of a PDA guy, but with Aubrey the urge to continually touch her was something he wasn't about to deny. "But I'd lose the chance to kiss you under a waterfall or save you from a shark or something."

"There are no waterfalls on the island," she said as she snuggled closer, her hand landing on his thigh just above his knee. "And if Jaws came to take me out I'd happily shove you into danger so I could swim away."

"That's cold."

She shot him a shit-eating grin as the boat pulled up to the island dock. "It's good you realize what kind of woman you've hooked up with on this trip."

"A very sexy one." He gave her a soft, quick kiss before they got up and followed the rest of the crowd to the stairs leading off the boat.

From their spot on the top row, it was easy to get the lay of the land. The island was set up with a beach area covered in lounge chairs placed close together and mostly occupied, an open shopping area with little grass huts filled with tourist tchotchkes, food stands, a guy with a cart selling pina coladas in coconut shells, and—bingo!—a small building where they could rent snorkeling gear.

"You in?" he asked, pointing to the building.

"Most definitely. How else am I going to shove you in the shark's way so I can sell my story and see it get made into a streaming-only movie?" Her face paled and her grip on his hand tightened as they made their way down to the single set of stairs and out onto the dock. "I didn't mean that."

"I didn't think you did, Aubrey." He pulled her close, sneaking another kiss as the other passengers swerved around them. "Now, on the other hand, *I* could definitely enact that plan and only to save you and therefore be a real life hero. The media coverage would be amazing." His smartwatch buzzed.

Glancing down, he saw his brother's name cross the caller ID. He hit decline call and walked with Aubrey away from the boat. The buzzing started again almost immediately. Fuck. Byron would not stop calling. It wasn't in his brother's DNA to give up when he was on a mission.

"I gotta take this real quick while I can still pick up signal from the ship."

"No worries." She squeezed his hand before letting go. "I'll go get our snorkel gear."

She strutted off and it took Carter two tries to get his Bluetooth headphones in because he was distracted by her hips swaying from side to side as she followed the wood plank path to the snorkel shop.

"Hey, what's up?"

"Your cover's been blown and Allyson is very not happy about it," Byron said, ignoring any socially-acceptable pleasantries per usual.

The Allyson was Allyson Hernandez as in the director of the movie he was desperately trying to get cast in. Fuck. This was not good.

"Give me all of it," he said, moving closer to the end of the dock in order to be as close to the ship as possible.

"It was that stupid fan account again," Bryon said, his frustration obvious. "Somehow they heard you were on board. The post was deleted but not before it was splashed all over everywhere. I swear to God, I'm going to track down whoever is behind the account and follow them around for a week to see how they like it."

Part bulldog, part agent, and part overprotective

brother, Byron had always been like this. Him picking on Carter was fine. Someone else? Not even a little bit.

"That's called stalking, Byron, the law frowns upon it."

"Not if you're the press," his brother groused.

"Which you're not, so settle back a little. How bad is it?" This was the part that made Carter's gut clench.

The window for being able to make a brand change in Hollywood was infinitesimal. If he missed this window and took another big budget action flick, he'd be doing only those movies for the rest of his career. They were fun, he enjoyed them, and he was grateful as hell for having the opportunities he did because of The Admiral movies, but he wanted career growth too. For that to happen he had to make a change.

"Well," Byron said, drawing out the four-letter word. "They deleted the post, which thank God didn't have an actual photo of you on the ship, but it had already gone viral by the time it was removed for whatever reason. I told you going off the grid would just make people hungrier for more details about your life."

"I had to have time to change my hair, get the fake tan, and do the rest." He watched blue water that seemed to go on forever knowing it all looked the same on the surface, but underneath it was a totally different story. "It's a process."

"Actors." Byron let out a huff. "You're all a pain in the ass."

"You've been telling me I'm a pain in the ass since I was twelve."

"And I've never been wrong."

"So what's the bottom line? Were you able to alleviate Allyson's concerns?"

Nervous? Him? Fuck yes.

"You don't pay me fifteen percent because I'm shitty at

my job," Byron shot back. "I'm cautiously optimistic this hasn't thrown your audition in the garbage disposal but if anything else pops up, your cover gets blown, she's going to pull back. She does not want the movie to be a media circus. She's not looking for a movie star for this part, she wants an actor. If you can't pull this off, she'll never believe you can't pull off carrying this movie." His brother paused, then continued, a thick ribbon of worry winding through his words, "Just don't get distracted and lose sight of what's at stake here. You want to make this career pivot that will change everything? You've got to commit. Eye on the prize."

"Any other clichés you want to throw my way?" Carter asked, desperate to change the mood from edge-of-the-world-disaster to the usual things-are-fucked-but-we'll-be-okay.

"Yeah." Byron chuckled. "You owe me, brother."

"Always."

Per usual, Byron ended the call without a goodbye. Chewing over the situation, Carter pocketed his headphones and made his way over to where Aubrey stood with two sets of flippers and snorkels.

"Everything okay?" she asked, cocking her head to one side.

"Yeah, just some work stuff." He reached over and snuck in another a quick kiss. "You ready to go see some fish?"

She grinned up at him. "I'm always up for fun."

And she had been since he first spotted her stealing her best friend's pants. It was something he'd forgotten about in the always-on world of Hollywood. Even a day off wasn't a day off because it was always about being seen in order to position himself in the best light for the next role. Shit, even this trip was just a fake. It wasn't a vacation, it was work.

But with Aubrey, it didn't feel that way, everything felt right, and that wasn't something he was ready to give up when they finally docked back in New York.

_____

Standing in the ocean nearly elbow to elbow with the thirty members of a singles support group while wearing a snorkel mask did not seem like the best place to tell Carter about her thirst account. Still, not telling him while they were out having fun and he kept smiling at her was like walking around with pebbles in her shoes.

Straightening her shoulders, she tried to stand solid even as the current was tugging her this way and that on the sandy bottom. "Carter, I have to tell you something."

He looked past her shoulder and grimaced. "Is it about that guy peeing off the rocks?"

"What?" She whipped around to look in the direction he'd motioned toward because he had to be joking.

Nope.

He was not.

A man in a T-shirt that said "Ride Me All The Way Home" had a coconut shell with a polka dotted tropical drink umbrella in one hand and his dick in the other. The spray was as strong as one of those Cupid fountains if the water had been turned on full blast. It was both appalling and impressive at the same time.

"He must have been holding that for a while," Carter said.

"I'm not feeling the snorkel thing anymore." Yeah, there was no getting past the fact that she was standing in that same ocean the dude was peeing into. "You wanna grab some food instead?"

"Sure."

They held hands as they wound their way through the tightly packed maze of chaise lounges toward the buffet under a pavilion. There were about a million different kinds of food all brought from the ship's kitchens. They each grabbed a plate and started down the line.

"Going home after this is going to wreck me," Aubrey said as she filled her plate. Comfort eating? Her? Absolutely. "There's no way microwaved seafood lasagna will ever taste the same as the fresh stuff."

"You don't cook?"

"Not unless forced." She followed Carter to a table where there were two open seats at an otherwise crowded table. "Believe me I was the last person anyone ever expected to take over gran's bakery."

"Who does the cooking there?"

"Ben, but he'd rather eat his own toes than deal with anything business or front-of-the-house related." People were definitely not Ben's thing. Leave him alone to create magic in the kitchen and all was good. Force him to talk to someone and it was like the man forgot every single bit of the manners his mama had taught him. Surly didn't even begin to cover it.

Carter's jaw tensed. "So you two make a good team."

"We make it work."

"What else is your life like back home?" He reached out, tangling his fingers in hers. "Tell me about Salvation."

Her senses going all jittery under his touch, it was hard to remember a damn thing about the town where she'd lived almost her entire life.

Pull it together, Aubrey!

"Well it's a small town but we're located in a sweet spot close to the cities for visitors yet far enough away that rent isn't out of reach." Oh yeah, way to really sell it. "We have the Sweet Salvation Brewery that's won all sorts of awards, a fantasy baseball camp every summer, and the world's best pecan pie."

He smoothed the tension off his face and brushed a kiss across her knuckles. "I'll have to visit."

She laughed loud enough to gain the attention of everyone at their table and immediately regretted it. Dropping her volume, she leaned in close. "Uh-huh, sure. It seems just the kind of vacation a guy like you would take." When every other single option in the world had been exhausted.

Carter cocked his head to the side. "A guy like me?"

"Yep, hot, single, and looking for a small town where there is exactly one honky tonk to grab a beer. It's very exciting." If it was Opposite Day.

"I hear the woman who runs the shuffleboard table at that bar has a great ass." He kissed the tips of her fingers one by one. "Anyway, maybe I can sweet talk her into giving me lessons."

"Oh my Lord, you two," said the woman next to them who had three empty coconut shells in front of her and the remains of three shredded drink umbrellas surrounding them. "I'm about to melt over here. I don't suppose you're looking for a third?"

"Not today," Carter said.

She sighed and shrugged. "Pity."

After finishing up with lunch, they made their way over to the touristy shops where they checked out all the offerings. While they stood side by side wearing funny hats, it was hard not to look at Carter and imagine what this would be like if it was just a regular Saturday afternoon back home at the monthly flea market. Just being a couple of goofs together. In all her time spent running the thirst account, it had never been about Carter Hayes the possible partner, but now it was hard to look at him and not imagine that.

Realization landed like a bad joke, it sucked all the air out of the room and left her wanting to crawl into a dark hole. She didn't just lust after him, he wasn't just a distraction from the basic drudgery of her life, she liked him, and it would be so easy for it to be more than just that.

She had to tell him about the thirst account, explain that it had all been done in good fun. She had to let him know that she posted about seeing him on board but that she'd deleted it as soon as she could. With any luck he'd see it as just being a silly blip in his life. It wasn't like he wasn't used to it and it wasn't like it changed the way he lived his daily life. Hell, he probably had no idea the account even existed. She'd tell him, feeling like a total fangirl dork. He'd laugh. It would be fine. Fine.

Rationalize much, Aubrey?

Damn. She hated it when her grown up self was right.

That formerly awe-inspiring seafood lasagna swirled uncomfortably in her stomach. "Carter, I gotta tell you something."

He put back the cruise-ship-shaped hat he was wearing, tugged her behind one of the shop huts, and leaned in close as if they were sharing a secret. "Is it about how you've decided we should get matching tattoos?"

Despite the general seasickness she was feeling even though she was on dry land, she had to chuckle at that idea. "Nope. It's—"

"Is it about how you want to catch the next boat back to the ship because you want to see if we can fit the both of us in that teeny-tiny shower?"

"That is never going to happen. I can barely fit in it by

myself." They were literally built to fit a ten year old and that was it. "I need to tell you something."

He dipped his head lower so his lips were millimeters from her earlobe. "Is it that you have a boyfriend?"

She shook her head, trying to maintain her sanity while her whole body was buzzing from being so close to him. He laid his hands lightly on her waist, not moving her closer but definitely making her heart rate shoot up.

"A husband?"

Another shake of her head because forming words was getting close to impossible.

He kissed the sensitive spot right behind her earlobe. "You're part of a monogamous polyamorous relationship and you've broken their trust and can't see me anymore?"

Desire warm and thick pulled at her, making her thinking fuzzy and her need to touch him greater.

"Then let's wait." He kissed a spot halfway down her neck. "Serious stuff later." He toyed with the knot holding her sarong in place. "Let's just enjoy this because I gotta tell you, I haven't had this much fun with someone in a long time."

Aubrey hadn't either. Fun wasn't really part of her life anymore. It was like until she'd hooked back up with her best friends from college, she'd forgotten she could. It wasn't that her life in Salvation was that bad, it was just that it wasn't how she'd planned for her life to go and some bitter little part of herself had let that fester and grow. What an asshole she'd been. She spent her days surrounded by sugar and family—who she loved—so what if she wasn't hanging out in cafes in Paris or dancing in penthouses? It was past time she stopped feeling sorry for herself for having a good life that just happened to be different than what she'd expected. It was time to grow up.

"I love it when you get that look on your face," he said, shooting her a cocky grin. "It means you've realized I'm right and that we should head back to the ship and not come out of our room until tomorrow."

She was holding on to her control by a thread here. "We are going to have to have a talk though."

"Another day," he agreed, nuzzling her neck. "Today I have plans for that sweet mouth of yours."

Then he kissed her and it scattered all of her best intentions to the four winds. Whatever it was about Carter that did this to her, she couldn't get enough of it and that made giving in so much easier. They'd talk—they would—and she'd tell him everything but not today. Today, she'd pretend that what she was really starting to want could come true and she could be with him as if all of this wasn't going to end in a few days when they got back to New York. She wasn't ready for that. She wasn't sure she ever would be.

NINE

There were worse things than waking up to soft sunlight filtering in through the teeny-tiny stateroom window wrapped in the arms of a man Aubrey was still asleep enough to think she might be falling for.

Who are you bothering to lie for, Aubrey Dean? You are falling. You have done fallen. Past tense. Waaaaaay past tense.

Why did it suck so hard when her inner bitch was right?

Carter tightened his grip while his fingertips danced over the curve of her hip. "Does that groan mean you can't believe we slept through dinner either?"

"Oh shit." She planted her hand on his chest and shoved herself up into a sitting position, guilt hitting her like an ice-packed snowball to the face. "Liv's note said we were supposed to meet everyone for dinner."

Seriously, hanging out with her best friends since college had been her entire reason for going on this cruise. And instead of doing that, she'd stolen all of Grace's pants, ditched her friends to hang out with a hot guy—one she was lying to by omission—and she'd missed dinner again.

She crumpled back into bed, plopped the pillow over her head, and let out a groan of pure I'm-the-asshole misery. "I'm the worst friend ever."

Carter plucked the pillow out of her grasp before she could smother herself and grinned down at her. Damn her mutinous heart, it did a flippity flop thing before settling into a steady rhythm again. What was it about him that made it seem as if it was going to be okay?

He brushed a strand of hair from her face. "I can score tickets to dinner at the captain's table before the cruise is over for everyone to make up for it."

"Wouldn't a special ask like that blow your cover?" Yeah, the one he really needed because of her.

"Not if I do it right—or more correctly, not if I have my brother Byron do it right." Staying propped up on his forearms, he dipped his head down and gave her a quick kiss. "He can name drop you as an up and coming bakery owner about to hit it big with a Netflix reality TV special."

"That's both devious and brilliant." And way too nice. "I can't ask you to do that."

"You're not asking, I'm offering." He dropped a trio of kisses along her jawline. "After all, you saving me is the reason why you're not hanging out with your friends."

Her gut twisted as she looked up at him. "That's not the whole story."

"Then I'm insisting," he said. "I'm not going to take no for an answer."

God, she was the worst. "Carter, we need to talk."

"Tonight, after dinner. Now we need to get moving so we don't miss out on Nassau completely. I wanna go do the most touristy things possible with you."

"Definitely tonight." *Girl, you are weak.* It was true. She couldn't even deny it. When it came to Carter, she lost the ability to think clearly. "I just hope dinner with the captain helps make up for me being such a flake so far. No offense, hot guy, but we're going to be spending a lot of time as we go back up to New York with Benjamin and the girls."

"We, huh?" He got up, rubbing his hands over his hard abs, and stood at the end of the bed still totally naked from the night before.

Oh, honey. That view could make a girl dumb.

It took her a second, but she finally remembered how to form words as she got up and made her way to the door connecting their rooms. "Yep, you're stuck with me for the rest of the cruise."

"And after?" There was something in the rough timbre of his voice that gave it a raw edge.

She didn't turn around to look at him. She couldn't. His question had suddenly began to matter too much to her. "What if I'm not exactly who you think I am? That would change things."

"So you're really a space alien?"

"Damn." She laughed, the tension seeping out of her and she finally pivoted to look at him. "You figured out my secret."

"Hustle up," he said, grabbing his towel and heading toward his bathroom. "Nassau awaits. We'll drop off notes for everyone about dinner on our way down to the dock."

Before jumping into the shower, Aubrey wrote four notes apologizing for missing dinner and promising to show up tonight with some surprise news. Fingers crossed Carter would be able to get them invites to the captain's table. If not, she'd be hoping whatever souvenirs she found in Nassau would help make up for her disappearing act.

Maybe she'd invite everyone down to Salvation for the annual Sweet Salvation Brewery open house and celebration this fall.

By the time they were both ready and had slid the notes under everyone's doors before walking off the ship, a smattering of people were already making their way back from Nassau. The crew members warned them to watch their time as she and Carter checked out of the ship and walked out into the bright sunshine of Nassau.

"So what do you want to do?" Carter asked as they walked down the dock, already holding hands.

"You want to start with the Queen's Staircase?" The Smitty-six step historical site was a literal staircase carved directly into the limestone." Then there are some local art galleries within walking distance we could explore."

"Sounds good." They passed through the area filled with cruise ship crew members who had been helping to direct the tourists but were now packing up their pamphlets. "Let's grab lunch, do the staircase and galleries. Then, maybe, we can fit in the pirate museum too."

"Aye aye, matey," she said in her best pirate accent.

Tonight after dinner, she'd duct tape him to a lounge chair if she had to, but she was going to tell him everything about the thirst account and the post she'd made and deleted. Until then, she'd go forward as if there wasn't a countdown clock starting to echo in her heart.

One Jerk chicken and two cold beers later, Carter still couldn't motivate himself to get up from the table. Content wasn't a word that was usually part of his vocabulary but right now, sitting in this restaurant in Nassau with Aubrey sitting across from him telling him a story about the absolute legend of an old woman who ran the local diner in Salvation and kept everyone in line with slices of unbelievably good pecan pie, he was. Sure, it could be because of the island breeze and that away-from-it-all bubble of being on a cruise but it wasn't. It was all Aubrey.

She stopped in the middle of a story about how Ruby Sue had fairy godmothered the Sweet triplets, who own a brewery in town, into their current relationships and shook her head.

"Sorry," she said. "I've talked your ear off about people you don't even know."

He shrugged, taking a sip of beer. "I liked it."

She blushed as she looked down at her lap, a smile tugging at her lips as if she couldn't quite believe what he'd said, but he'd meant it. He liked listening to her talk, liked her laugh, liked the way her devious little mind worked when it came to pranks, liked how she was game for anything, and he loved the way she felt underneath him when she came. Now wasn't the time to tell her, because he didn't want to sound like a creeper, but there was no way he was walking away from the possibility of being with her when the ship docked. He'd been on too many movie sets and been a part of too many relationships that happened because people were stuck in the same far flung location to not realize it was different with Aubrey.

"Come on," she said, getting up from her chair. "Let's go see those steps."

The walk from the restaurant to the Queen's Staircase wasn't far but they got turned around a couple of times and ended up popping into a few souvenir shops and an art gallery. By the time they got to the staircase, it was practically deserted. Arm around Aubrey's waist, tucking her close to him because *not* touching her seemed impossible, they listened to the local guide who explained that between 1793 and 1794, slaves carved sixty-six steps out of the limestone to provide direct access to Fort Fincastle. The staircase was renamed in the 1800s for Queen Victoria, who abolished slavery when she ascended to the throne. Looking at the walls, covered in tropical foliage and smoothed by time, the landmark of harsh beauty was as awe inspiring as it was painful to imagine the circumstances of its building.

Once the guide finished, Carter hung back at the bottom of the staircase to make a quick phone call while Aubrey made her way up the steps, pausing to take photos of the palm trees set against the steps and the waterfall about halfway up.

"I need a favor," he said as soon as his brother answered the phone.

Byron hurumphed. "I need my own private island."

"You have a private island." It was a short helicopter ride from where he stood right now.

"But I share it with you," Byron said with an over dramatic sigh playing up the poor-me melodrama that both of them knew he didn't mean.

"What a hard fucking life you lead," Carter said, laughing.

"So now that that is out of the way," Bryon said, going back to his normal business-first fast clip where each word came out quick because time was money. "What's the favor?"

"Can you somehow without alerting the cruise ship company that I'm who I am, arrange dinner with the captain for ten?" The way Aubrey's shoulders had fallen and the expression of regret on her face back on the ship had eaten away at him all day. He hadn't kidnapped her or anything, but she'd upended her plans for the cruise to help him and he needed to make that up to her.

"You making friends?"

"It's Aubrey's friends," Carter said, watching as she leaned close to the staircase wall to capture a detail with her cellphone camera. "So Liv, Grace, Benjamin, and Kendall along with their plus ones—and Aubrey and me, of course."

"Aubrey?" Byron asked, his tone deceptively calm. "Her last name wouldn't happen to be Dean would it?"

Unease shot through him like a rocket blast, making him wince. Carter knew that tone. It was the same one his brother had used whenever he went into protective agent mode. The result was usually a lot of groveling and a couple of more million thrown his way by whoever had chosen poorly and crossed Byron Hayes.

"Yeah," he said and then fought hard not to give into the anxiety squeezing his lungs. "How did you know her last name?"

"Because I'm staring a file containing her photo right now."

That didn't make sense. None of this made sense. "What's going on, Byron?"

"She's the person behind that damn Instagram account, the one who posted that you were on the cruise and nearly ruined everything—she still could."

"No, it couldn't be." He glanced back at Aubrey. She smiled at him, her cell phone camera facing him, and waved. There wasn't a flash, but that didn't mean she hadn't taken a photo. Had she been documenting their every move, is that what she had to tell him before? "It's gotta be a different person."

"Yeah, that's likely," Byron scoffed. "Blonde hair. Huge

koi tattoo on her ribs? Looks like she'd melt if you put her in your mouth—of course you've probably already done that and know for sure."

His grip tightened on his phone until the corners ate into his palm. "Fuck you, Byron."

"Don't hate on the messenger. The good news is that we have the identity now and I'm working to get the Insta account shut down. Copyright violations or something, I don't know Fred will come up with some scary bullshit to put in a cease and desist. All you have to do is stay clear of that woman from now on."

The pronouncement still hit like a sucker punch. Carter knew his brother was right even if he wanted more than anything for it all to be a misunderstanding too many things suddenly made sense. There were too many coincidences. Had she arranged to have a connecting room? Had the pants theft just been a rouse to get his attention? Were her friends in on it? How much were the gossip sites willing to pay for the photos? Was all of it bullshit?

A dark, swirling anger as the inevitable realization exams too tangible to ignore made his entire body tense as he watched Aubrey. "We're in Nassau together."

"Then get back to the ship and ditch her," Byron all but yelled into the phone. "Remember what's at stake here, Carter. What's more important, some chick you met on a singles cruise or the role of a lifetime?"

He stared at his phone after his brother hung up without a goodbye, per usual, and tried to unwind the emotions twisting him up. Part of him wanted—needed—to believe it wasn't right, that Byron had gotten it wrong. But that wasn't possible. His brother was a lot of things, but he was damn good at his job and he was thorough. There's no way he would have named Aubrey without a solid, air-tight case.

Carter looked up to where she stood about a third of the way up the limestone staircase. She paused to take a photo of the waterfall next to stairs and then turned around and waved at him again. He didn't wave back. He couldn't. He was having too much trouble catching his breath after that gut punch. She hesitated for a moment, then headed down to him.

"Everything okay?" she asked.

And the concern in her voice as she took his hand, that all too familiar buzz of awareness shot through him at her touch, had him rethinking the truth again. Was he really this gullible? Or was there more to all of this than he or Byron knew? God, the whole thing made his head feel like it was going to explode.

"We need to get back to the ship," he said.

Once there, he'd figure this all out. He'd get the truth from Aubrey and after that he had no fucking clue.

She looked down at her clock on her phone. "Oh shit!" She turned the screen to face him. "How is it that late?"

Adrenaline jolted him into motion. They took off at a sprint. Backtracking their path back to the port should have been easy, but that wasn't how it worked out. After at least five wrong turns, they got there right in time to see the ship heading home without them.

"What do we do now?" Aubrey asked, her eyes wide with panic.

Wasn't that the question he couldn't get out of his head. "I'm getting a hotel room and then we're going to have a talk and you're going to tell me everything."

Because that discussion sure as hell wasn't one that could take place in the open. He wasn't about to have his cover completely blown by having a fight with Aubrey in the middle of the Nassau cruise ship port where any tourist with a camera could document the entire thing and sell it to the highest bidder. He took her hand and started toward the hotel they'd passed a few blocks ago.

"Carter, what's going on?" She asked, taking a step and half to every one of his long, fast strides.

"We'll talk about it at the hotel."

"No." She tugged her hand free and stopped walking. "You need to tell me right now."

He turned, the white noise of his hurt and anger rushing in his ears and blocking out the sound of the ocean, the people passing them on the sidewalk, and everything else in the world except Aubrey. He heard her perfectly and it cut right through him that she was still playing the innocent. She wasn't dumb. She had to have guessed the gig was up, but she couldn't let go. Whatever the payoff was, it had to be significant.

"I know you were the one running that damn thirst account that said I was on the cruise."

She took a step toward him, reaching for him. "I can explain."

He sidestepped her easily and started walking again. "Not here."

And as they made their way at a fast clip to the hotel, he pushed down the part of him that still hoped there was an explanation for all of this. He couldn't afford to let that happen, he'd been fooled by her already once and he couldn't let that happen again.

TEN

Aubrey was fighting to hold it together when she walked through the hotel room door and into the suite with its three walls of windows overlooking the hotel's private beach. At any other time she would have rushed over to the panoramic view of the Nassau Harbor to look out at the gorgeous Caribbean water and sent up a thankful prayer that there had been a hotel room left at the last minute.

Not this time.

It was all she could do to even glance over at the early evening view. All she could do was watch Carter as he strode over to the desk and set the room keys down with deliberate care, each move precise and controlled. Then, he stalked over to the window stared out at the harbor, his entire body tense.

She stood her ground near the door, wanting to give him his space. "I know you're mad, but I can explain."

He didn't bother to turn around. "Can't wait to hear it."

The ice in his voice pelted her and she flinched. What had she been expecting? She'd known it would go like this and, honestly, this was why she'd waited. She'd been a giant chicken putting off the inevitable because she wasn't ready for this, she wasn't ready to lose Carter.

Exhaling a deep breath, she straightened her shoulders and look him straight in the back of the head. If he wouldn't turn around, fine, but it was past time she finally got the truth out. "The thirst account, it's for fun, I never meant it to hurt you. It was just a hobby, a silly thing. It doesn't mean anything. No one is just one thing. I can be the woman who started a dumb Insta account and the one who fell for the last man she ever expected to meet."

"Really?" He turned around, his hands were shoved into his pockets and his face blank of all expression as if they were talking about the weather or how long to microwave a day old glazed donut. "That post could fuck my entire career path." His voice held steady, as calm as the water in the harbor. "I'd say that means something."

The casual dismissal in his tone, set her on edge but she bit it back, fighting to keep the emotion out of her voice. Losing control right now would not help. "I didn't know when I posted it and by the time I figured it out, it was already everywhere."

He chuckled. It was not a nice sound. "How convenient."

"Not really, not at all," she said, her voice breaking as she blinked back tears. "Once I met you, got to know you, having the post, the account seemed weird." She took a step toward him, arm outstretched, as if physical contact could make him understand that none of this had been malicious. "I never meant to hurt you."

The absolute ice cold fury in his expression stopped her dead in her tracks and her gut dropped. It was too late. It had been from the beginning and she should have known that but she let herself believe that there could be more. It had been a pretty dream, but it had never been real.

"That's what you think I'm so pissed about?" Carter crossed his arms over his chest as if he had to contain himself. "That you had a damn fan account?" He let his head fall back and let out a hard laugh, then continued his voice rising with each word. "Of all the— I'm *pissed* because you could have told me and you didn't. You *knew* how much this role meant. I *told* you." Pausing, he rubbed the back of his head and pursed his lips together, obviously trying to pull back. When he started speaking again, his voice was quiet and heavy with resignation. "And you kept silent—even after the post was deleted."

"I wanted to tell you—I tried—but you didn't want to listen." She wasn't innocent here, but she had tried to tell him. "Every time I started, you changed the subject or kissed me."

"Of course," he said smacking his palm against his forehead. "It's *my* fault you didn't tell me. But what does it matter?" He closed the distance between them, stopping just short of touching. "We were just fucking."

An angry heat rushed up from the pit of her stomach, rushing through her like a wildfire because that was not true —at least not for her and she would have sworn not for him either. "Is that all this was to you?"

His gaze dipped down to her mouth and then away, a bitter smile twisting his lips. "Don't pretend you ever thought of it as something beyond a way to gain more visibility for your Insta."

"Damn it." Heart racing, she cupped his face in her palms, forcing him to look at her, as she rose to her tiptoes desperate to make him understand. "What's between us is more than just some stupid thirst account. I'm falling for you."

"Very convincing." He turned his head, kissing her palm. "I almost believe that but we both know it's nothing but lust."

"Carter, you know that's not true."

Aubrey dropped her hands, but it was too late. The sensual pull of being this close to him, the touch of his lips still buzzing against her hand, the way her body was still so attuned to his as if she could feel his touch before he even reached for her—all of it wound its way through her, making her overwhelmingly aware of how much she ached for him.

"Do I?" He came in close, holding back on touching her as if giving her a final out, one he knew there was no way she wanted to take. "I wish I did."

Aubrey held her breath as the world stopped in that moment, the one when anything could happen. She could walk away now or she could try, one last time, to make him understand. The thing was, there wasn't a choice. She leaned up and kissed him, putting everything she had into it hoping he'd recognize the truth in her touch.

He pulled back, but there was no missing the hard tension in his body or the desire darkening his eyes.

"This isn't going to change anything," he said, his voice a rough rumbling jumble of need and want.

"If that's true, then why are you scared to touch me?"

"You want me to touch you?" He took her by the hips and pressed backward, backing her up against the wall and lifted her up so she fit perfectly against his hard cock. "You want this, Aubrey?"

She didn't hesitate. "Yes."

This was a mistake, but there was no way Carter could walk out of here without touching Aubrey again. Yeah, he was probably being an idiot but part of him couldn't let go, not yet anyway.

He brushed his thumb over her slightly parted mouth. She shivered and nipped his thumb. Giving in to the wicked temptation she offered, he lowered his mouth to hers in a demanding kiss, melding his lips to hers, not waiting for an invitation to sink his tongue into her luscious mouth. Dragging his hands upward from her hips, he lifted her sundress higher as he went until he had to pull away from her to pull it over her head and fling it across the room. He'd no more than done that than he dipped his head back down, feasting on her mouth as he plastered his hungry body against her, rocking against her even though the friction wasn't nearly enough. He wanted—needed—more.

He wanted to watch her tits sway as she rode him until she couldn't come anymore, have her fall into a sweaty heap beside him to sleep, and then wake up a few hours later to do it all again and again and again. Fuck. Was there anything more dangerous than that? Easing back from her, he fought to steady his breathing and get the world back on an even keel. Fucking to prove a point, that's all this was. It's all it ever could be.

He rocked his dick against the crotch of her soaked panties, slow and steady, so unlike his heartbeat. He didn't seek out her kiss-swollen mouth, instead he zeroed in on the base of her throat, sucking and nipping at the sensitive flesh then licked his way up her throat, bringing his mouth against her ear.

"Do you feel how fucking hard I am for you?" He ground his cock against her, squeezing her ass cheeks in his firm grip. "This is what you do to me every time I so much as think about you and it's only been a few days. I guess I should be grateful. A few months, years, with you and I'd be lost."

She stiffened in his arms. "Put me down."

He stilled against her, their position as intimate as it could be with her still in panties and him still in his jeans. *Way to go asshole. How about you keep your jerk mouth closed unless someone writes the lines for you?* He knocked his forehead against the wall but released his hold.

She glided down his body until her feet touched the carpet and pushed him back several paces so that the back of his knees nearly hit the bed. Not giving him time to recover, she swept her leg behind his and knocked him down onto the Snow White comforter.

"Just fucking, huh?" Her hands were on the button of his jeans, flicking it open with ease. "Is that all there is between us?" She yanked down his zipper and shoved down his jeans and boxers. "Fine. Then let's fuck. One more for the road, right?"

He lay flat on his back, never moving a muscle while she stripped him, turned on beyond belief, her ferocity making his balls ache. And as she stood, looking down at him as she slipped off her bra, he deliberately slid his right hand across his pecs, over the flat landscape of his abs and stopped only when he wrapped his long fingers around the base of his shaft, rubbing his cock in long, slow strokes.

Watching him, she cupped her tits and rolled her hard nipples. "I will miss seeing you do that."

"You like watching me jerk off?"

"Almost as much as I like this." She strutted to the edge of the bed, lowered herself, and planted her knees on either side of his thighs before wrapping her hands around his wrists and bringing them up over his head. She ran her hands down his arms, keeping herself positioned so that her center hovered directly above his hard cock but didn't touch it. It was fucking torture. Without hardly any effort he could pull his arms free, flip her, and sink balls deep inside her, but there was something about the way she was looking at him right now — half in awe and half out of her mind — that made him want to find out what she'd do next. He didn't have to wait long. She lowered her head to his pecs and lapped at his flat, dusky nipple, drawing him into her mouth and sucking.

His moan echoed in the room, and he bucked against her just enough to bring his dick into direct contact with her.

She clicked her tongue against the back of her teeth. "I don't think so. Not yet anyway."

Still holding his arms in place, she scooted higher over him, kissing her way up across his shoulders and up his neck, teasing him within millimeters of losing all control.

"Just." She brushed her lips across his but pulled away before it developed into a real kiss. "Fucking."

He practically heard glass shattering at that moment when his control broke. Slipping free of her hold, he moved his hands to her round hips, rolled her over, and settled himself between her splayed legs and bent down to take her mouth with an intensity that shook him to the core. His tongue swept inside her mouth, teasing her until she was writhing beneath him, her busy hands gliding over his thighs to his ass and urging him wordlessly to move against her. On this point, they were in agreement. He lowered himself until his cock lay nestled against her core, her damp panties the only thing between him and her pussy's slick tight grip.

His hands were everywhere at once, caressing her tits, skimming across her stomach, and finding their way between her panties and her silky folds. He dipped a finger into her entrance, his thumb circling her attention-starved clit as her wanton moan filled the hotel room. The sound reached somewhere deep and primal inside him, but he wanted to push her, make sure she always remembered this, remembered him.

He dipped his head lower, taking the elastic band of her panties between his teeth and dragging them down her legs. Pushing her legs back open as wide as they could go, he kissed and licked his way up her calves and thighs, not stopping until he arrived at her slick entrance.

"Say it, Aubrey," he said, his words pressing up against her swollen flesh as his tongue and fingers worked in concert.

"Say what?"

God, that breathy about-to-come tremor in her voice nearly killed him, but he had to do this. He had to prove the point. "That this is just fucking. That it doesn't mean anything."

"You're an asshole, Carter."

"Yes." He felt her tighten against him, so close to coming and he stopped, stilling right as she was on the edge. "Say it anyway."

"It's just fucking."

Like a gullible fool, he would have sworn he heard a catch in her voice but he knew better. She'd lied to him for the entire cruise. Why stop now? He sure as hell wasn't. Renewing his efforts, he lapped at her clit and worked his fingers inside her, focused on making her come so he could block the rest of it out. Then, her muscles locked and she came undone.

Her taste still on his lips, he leaned back and grabbed his jeans, pulled a condom from his wallet, and unrolled it over his cock as he watched her come down from her orgasm. He wouldn't forget the sight. Her blonde hair fanned around her as she looked up at him with that dazed, satisfied look in her eyes. It was almost enough to make him forget. God knew, he wanted to because Aubrey was right, this had never been just fucking.

And when he sank into her, slowly inch by inch until he filled her completely, he knew that for all of this being a way to make her remember him that he'd be the one who'd never forget. Fuck she felt so good, so tight and hot around him and he gave into the moment. Forgetting everything before and after as he thrust into her again and again, reaching down between them to roll his thumb over her straining clit. It didn't take long to put him on the edge as she rose up to meet his every stroke.

"Aubrey I—"

He had no idea what he would have said after that because her orgasm hit hard, his name on her lips as she tightened around his dick and he came with her.

Catching his breath as he held her in his arms still riding high, it wasn't so much an epiphany as an acceptance that struck him. Whatever had happened, whatever had gone down, they had to figure this out. She'd fucked up. He'd fucked up. But together, they could make it right.

"Aubrey," he said, rolling over on his side so they could talk face to face.

Shit.

Her eyes were closed and her breathing steady. Okay, it could wait. He'd get cleaned up, she'd get some sleep, and then they'd talk, straighten the whole thing out. He got up and went to the bathroom to do just that, but when he walked back out, Aubrey was gone.

The walk to the U.S. Embassy from the hotel was a short one but even if it had been across the island, Aubrey didn't think it would be long enough for her to pull herself together.

Everything hurt and it was her own fault. She'd stopped ugly crying in the hotel lobby bathroom so that was a bonus, but she doubted it made much difference considering the looks people were sending her way as she walked the couple of blocks to the embassy. She'd known from the beginning that the truth would come out but she'd let herself pretend it would all work out. She should know better. That only happened in the movies. Well The Admiral wasn't coming in to save the day in this one. By the time she got to the embassy, the entrance gate was shut and the sign on the front of the guard post said they wouldn't open again until the next morning.

It was all she could do not to crumble up into a ball right there on the sidewalk and cry. Fisting her hands, she sucked in a breath and tried to think. Falling apart now wouldn't help. She'd do that later when she got back to Salvation and the boring life in the bakery that was sounding better and better with each broken heartbeat.

An older man in a suit walking by paused in front of her. "Miss your cruise?" he asked, his American accent unmistakable.

"Yeah." She sucked in a deep breath, willing herself not to give in to the tears she'd been fighting back since she walked out of Carter's hotel room. "My friends are on board, I need to let them know I'm okay."

He cocked his head to the side, "And are you okay?"

Aubrey let out the sigh she'd been holding in so long that it ended with something that sounded a little too much like a whimper to her ears. "Not even close."

"You know what, why don't you come inside." He nodded at the guard who opened the gate for them. "We'll get you all straightened out with a temporary passport and on the next flight home."

"I thought it was closed for the night."

"Well," he said walking through the gate. "Every once in a while we observe Pacific Standard Time when the occasion calls for it, so we've got a few hours before it's five. Plus, being the ambassador has its privileges. Let's go get you taken care of and make sure your friends know you're okay."

She wouldn't be that, not for a good long time, but getting home and eating pecan pie at The Kitchen Sink Diner would help. She had to believe that because it was pretty much the only thing making it possible for her to get one foot in front of the other and put more distance between her and the man she'd fallen for who never wanted to see her again. And who could blame him? She'd fucked it all up from the beginning.

ELEVEN

B yron would be having a fit if he ever found out that Carter had voluntarily opted for coach to get the first flight out of Nassau and back to New York after a night spent walking around Nassau looking for Aubrey. It wasn't until he got to the embassy this morning for a temporary passport that he found out she'd already been there and left on the final flight out last night.

And that was that. He'd overreacted like an asshole and fucked it up. He should have listened to her at the very least. Instead he'd acted like a total douchebag and she'd walked out, which he realized this morning he rightly deserved.

Even though it wasn't enough, bypassing the wine drinkers in first class to fold himself into a smaller seat with pretty much negative legroom seemed at least some punishment. He was a fucking idiot.

He checked his ticket for the third time to confirm his row and seat as he did the slow shuffle down the aisle behind people trying to fit what should clearly be a checked bag into the overhead bin. One guy was telling with the airline attendant that there had to be something wrong with the bin on this plane because it had fit on the plane he'd taken down to Nassau. Judging by the what-kind-of-bullshit-are-you-slinging look on the woman's face, she wasn't buying it. Finally, the guy gave up and everyone snuck into whatever open space there was while he took the walk of shame back to the boarding area with his too-big bag.

Carter's seat was two rows further down. A woman and a skinny kid were already sitting down. The woman had her hair pulled back into a braid and was wearing the sunburn of a Michigan tourist who'd vacationed anywhere near the equator. The kid, who looked all of eight, was wearing one of those antiviral face masks and had dark circles under his eyes. The kid was by the window. The woman was on the aisle.

He hesitated, not sure what the protocol was in this situation.

"Shadron, time to get in your seat," the woman said, giving Carter a small apologetic smile. "This gentleman here has the window."

The boy let out a soft sigh without looking away from the window but started to get up.

"It's alright, I can take the middle seat. No big deal." Self-flagellation for the win? That's right.

"That's sweet of you, but it's okay," the woman said.

She got up and her son moved to the middle seat. Carter sat down by the window and tucked his arms as close to his sides as possible and settled back for a long ass flight back to New York. With any luck, he'd sleep through the whole damn thing and wouldn't dream about Aubrey even once.

It wasn't until they'd been airborne for a few minutes before he felt a little nub of a finger poking him in the arm. He cracked an eye open and looked at the kid on his left.

His many years of media training was the only thing keeping him from growling—right up until the kid shoved a folded piece of paper at him and gave him one of those weird, awkward kid winks that was more of a blink.

Hello, Admiral. My name is Shadron. I'm eight. Are you undercover?

Fuck. So much for his Bahama Living cap pulled down low and the days' worth of beard growth. He hadn't even fooled a little kid. He didn't have it in him to lie to a kid who was obviously sick. The best he could hope for was to keep his real identity between him and Shadron. He lowered his tray table, snagged the pencil from the boy, and jotted down a quick response.

I'm not at liberty to say.

The boy read the note, nodded, and started writing his response on the bottom. He adjusted the mask covering his mouth scrawled off a few words before handing it over.

Understood. You are my favorite superhero.

How often had Carter heard that from kids and adults during the past ten years of playing The Admiral? Too many to count. However, he heard the studio's PR person's voice telling him that while he may have heard it all before that it was the first time that fan had gotten to say it to him and that was what was important. He borrowed the pencil again and handed over his reply.

Thank you. It's a huge honor to meet you.

The boy grinned big enough that it was noticeable even with his mask and started to write another note. That's when Carter felt like he was being watched, he looked up and locked eyes with Shadron's mom who was staring at him with the kind of do-not-fuck-with-my-child glare that only a mom could give. Okay, maybe passing notes with a little kid without his mom's go-ahead didn't have the best optics. Before he could explain though, the kid slid over the note that now was covered with his uneven handwriting almost all the way down to the bottom. Carter held it up, angling it so the boy's mom could read it too.

Sir, I would like to ask a few questions. 1. Is Bolt really your best friend? 2. How long have you had your dog, Tug? 3. Are you worried about facing down Iceburg? He's the most powerful super villain on the planet.

Carter glanced over at the woman and raised an eyebrow in question. If she wanted to shut the conversation down, he would find a way to make that happen. However, as soon as she started reading the note, her suspicion turned to something softer and the tip of her nose got red as she pulled a Kleenex out of her pocket and mouthed, "Thank you."

Taking that for a go ahead, Carter started answering the kid's questions. And so it went for the next half hour, the writing back and forth until the kid's eyelids must have gotten too heavy to hold open any longer and he fell asleep, his dark eyelashes so long they brushed the top of his face mask.

"Thank you," Shadron's mom said with a sniffle. "I mean you probably were looking forward to your nap rather than pretending to be some Hollywood super hero."

"All in a day's work." Just usually against a green screen.

The woman let out a sigh. "He's gonna be telling the

nurses this story for days and I hope you don't mind but I just don't have the heart to explain that you aren't the real Carter Hayes."

He schooled his expression before he ruined his cover. "What gave it away?"

She waved her hands at their tight quarters. "Hello, coach section." Letting out a quiet chuckle that sounded rusty from disuse, she shook her head. "Those movies mean the world to him. Watching them is usually how he deals with all the time in the hospital, makes him feel as if he can conquer the cancer just like The Admiral beats all those super villains." Her chin trembled and she crumpled the tissue in her hand, visibly swallowing. "And he will. You take my word for it, he will." Exhaling a quick breath, she gave him a curt nod. "Now you've been kept from your nap long enough. I won't bother you anymore, I just had to say thank you."

Carter closed his eyes, but sleep didn't come. His brain was spinning out too much. For all the effort he'd put into shaking off The Admiral's persona because of how the role had limited what parts casting directors thought he'd work for, he'd never thought about what the character had meant to the people who paid to sit in the dark and watch The Admiral up on the big screen. How many other Shadrons were out there finding even a little bit of inspiration in a hero who guaranteed happy endings? And what kind of idiot was he for never seeing that?

You're a real asshole, Hayes.

Maybe there was a way to do both, to be The Admiral and to stretch his professional muscles. It didn't only have to be one or the other. He could make both happen. No one was just one thing.

Now, where did you hear that?

He gritted his teeth and forced himself off that path. No. He wouldn't think about her. Aubrey was gone and it was his fault. Best just to forget about her and finally get some shuteye before they landed in New York.

T wo days after getting home in the dead of night after snagging the last seat on the last flight away from the last man she should have fallen for, Aubrey was dragging ass. Not even the strong-enough-to-put-hair-on-a-person's-chest coffee at the bakery had perked her up. There was only one thing in all of Salvation that could help at that moment—Ruby Sue's pecan pie.

Feet filled with lead, she flipped the bakery sign to Closed and crossed the street to The Kitchen Sink Diner. Ruby Sue sat in her usual spot on a tall stool behind the cash register. Petite, sharp-eyed, and with a voice made raw from too many cigarettes for too long, Ruby Sue knew everything about everyone in Salvation thanks to her nosy nature and the fact that her pecan pie was worth giving up secrets for.

Ruby Sue took one look at Aubrey and got down off her stool and went to the pie case. "You look like you've been trampled by a herd of wild goats drunk on the Sweet's family moonshine."

"If only I felt as good as I looked." Aubrey sat down at one of the empty stools at the counter, thankful it was after the lunch rush and before the early bird dinner special so they were alone except for the cook/dishwasher, Otis, who was working on the crossword puzzle in the corner booth.

Ruby Sue took out a plate of pecan pie, one with extra goo spilling out from the crust, and sat it in front of Aubrey.

Then, she took out two forks and handed one over. "That sounds like the beginning of a story—one with a man. Hopefully, he has a butt I could bounce a quarter off of, if so please describe it in detail."

"Ruby Sue," she gasped, a fork full of pecan goodness stalled halfway to her mouth.

"What?" The older woman shrugged her bony shoulders. "I'm old, not missing the ability to admire a good butt."

"He has a world-class butt," she said before stuffing the pie in her mouth before she could say more.

There were, after all, entire Instagram sites devoted to his ass. Since she'd landed, she'd been avoiding social media. It just wasn't the same anymore. Her thirst site, the ones she followed, each one would be a smack-in-the-face reminder of the possibility of something amazing that she'd messed up.

"Excellent." Ruby Sue took a bite. "Now tell me that he has a brain and ambition too."

"He does."

"Wonderful. So what has you moping around looking like you ate your own donuts." Ruby Sue dropped her volume to a whisper. "No offense, but we all heard about your attempt to bake when you first moved back from college."

That had been a disaster. The volunteer firefighters had been nice about it though. Luckily no one had been hurt and the worst damage was a charbroiled tray of bear claws. This time it was much worse.

"I messed it all up." She set her fork down, the idea of taking another bite making her stomach roil. "I lied to him, well, at least by omission."

"Did you apologize?"

Aubrey nodded, tears already pooling in her eyes as the

image of Carter's face when he confronted her in the hotel room, his hurt as plain as the pecans on top of Ruby Sue's pie.

The older woman took another bite from their shared slice, chewing it slowly as she turned her assessing gaze on Aubrey. "Did you make amends?"

"I can't." She sank back against the chair, wishing she could just melt into it. "It's too big."

"The most important things always are." Ruby Sue finished off the pie, dumped the crumbs from the plate into the garbage, and then added the dish to the red tub waiting for Otis after he finished his puzzle. "Life doesn't just give you what you want. You have to fight for it."

"Yeah, but you also have to know when to accept reality." Like there was any actual hope of her ending up with a movie star. Even if she hadn't messed everything up by posting about how Carter was on the cruise, she was a wannabe writer working at her gran's bakery in a small town. It would have never worked out and so maybe it was for the best that he'd found out. Still, she couldn't even think his name without having to purse her lips together to keep from crying. "That's what I did when I came back here," she continued, her voice trembling. "I shelved my book proposal, set my alarm for o'dark thirty, and did what needed to be done."

Ruby Sue huffed at her. "At first maybe, but then you got comfortable and a bit lazy." She pointed a liver-spotted finger at Aubrey. "I've known you since you were a Daisy Scout and you walked in here during the lunch rush and sold me ten boxes of overpriced cookies despite the fact that I was trying to run the cash register, seat people, and eavesdrop on the latest town gossip. Growing up, there wasn't a single day when you sat back and just accepted things. You have too much spark to you to give that up now. It's still there, you just have to find it."

That's what Aubrey had thought she'd done on the cruise. She'd thought it was being with her friends and Carter, but that wasn't it. The cruise had forced her to take herself out of the rut she'd fallen into. The new perspective the cruise had given her was like having electricity running through her veins like she was in college again. She'd been inspired. She'd been happy. She'd been open enough to fall for Carter despite knowing in the long term there was no way to make it work.

Ruby Sue made an mmm-hmmm noise as she shot Aubrey an I-told-you-so-look that sent her gray eyebrows into the stratosphere. "I can practically see the lightbulb turning on above your head."

That's pretty much what it felt like, as if someone had flipped a switch. She didn't want to go back to feeling like she was just going through life by the motions again. She couldn't fix things with Carter but that didn't mean she couldn't keep that cruise perspective when it came to the rest of her life. It wasn't too late to still be that person she'd been before, the fun one who took chances and just went for it.

Mind whirling, she glanced over at Otis with his crossword. He was gnawing on his pencil just like she did when she was in the middle of research. Her heartbeat sped up.

"I know what I need to do." She hustled off the chair and toward the door. "I just have to figure out how."

"I've found pie always helps with that," Ruby Sue said, handing her a full pecan pie already wrapped up. "I've had this set aside, figuring you'd be over soon enough."

She gave the older woman a kiss on her papery-thin cheek. "You are the best."

"You think I don't know that?" Ruby Sue said with a chuckle.

Then Aubrey was off, striding down Main Street with purpose for the first time since she came home from college. She knew exactly what she was going to do next.

Carter couldn't stop fidgeting with the linen napkin as he sat in front of the indie film world's favorite director Allyson Hernandez. She wore head-to-toe black including a non-ironic beret that she somehow managed to carry off. He fiddled with the corner of the cream material as their waiter took Allyson's very specific order.

"And for you, sir?" the waiter asked, turning to Carter.

"The hot fudge sundae, please."

The waiter's eyebrow may have gone up a millimeter or two but otherwise he didn't have any outward reaction. "Very well."

"Interesting choice for brunch," Allyson said. "Gotta sweet tooth?"

"It's become a new favorite." Okay, so he'd had at least one hot fudge sundae each day since he'd returned because like a sap it reminded him of Aubrey and he couldn't help but poke that open wound that still hurt like hell. In fact, he'd spent most of the four days since he flew out of Nassau trying to distract himself from thinking about her by deep diving into the movie script. "It reminds me of..." A friend? A lover? The woman who got away because he was a dumb-ass? "It reminds me of someone."

The director made a non-committal huh and took a sip

of her water. "You know you weren't my first choice for this part."

"Probably not even the tenth," he said, practically on autopilot after spotting a woman across the restaurant that sent his pulse into overdrive.

He leaned forward in his chair, still facing the director but watching the woman just over Allyson's shoulder. Blonde hair. The right height. She was facing away from him and it took nearly everything he had not to bound out of his seat and rush over to her.

Allyson chuckled and gave a whatcha-gonna-do shrug. "No, but I have to admit you got me curious with the cruise challenge. It went off nearly without a hitch."

The woman turned around and Carter sank back against the plush back of his seat, his pulse returning to normal, and the ache in his chest that had been building since he walked out of the hotel bathroom and found Aubrey gone returned in full force that made him wince.

"You know what got me though?" Allyson continued, "It was the fact that you were willing to work for it, you didn't expect it to be handed to you. That's not always the case in our world. So tell me about the sundae."

The change in subject came so swiftly that he answered without thinking. "I met someone on the cruise."

"And she didn't know who you were?"

"She did." Hell, by the end she probably knew him better than anyone else but Byron. "She was the one who posted that I was on board, but I didn't know that until Nassau."

That gut punch still had him waking up in a cold sweat in the middle of the night with her name on his lips. God, he'd fucked it up. If he'd taken the time to think instead of just react he would have realized all of the times she'd tried to tell him.

"When did you find out?" Allyson asked.

"Not until it was too late and I was already neck deep with her." So basically from the moment she'd shoved those pants up his shirt and told him to play along.

"Conflict, I like it." Allyson clapped then rolled her eyes at him when he glared at her. "Oh don't look at me like that. We're in the business of telling stories, this is what we do. So what happened?"

He didn't mean to tell her, but everything spilled out. He explained how they'd met while she was stealing clothes from her best friend and had clicked immediately. Then, he filled her in on the shuffle board and the backstory game and the way being around Aubrey just seemed to make sense in a way that he hadn't felt before. The whole thing should have sounded idiotic when he put it out there in words to a stranger—one who had his career in her hands— but it didn't. It was just the truth.

"So where is she now?" Allyson asked after the waiter delivered their food.

"She flew home." Without him. Without saying goodbye.

And you blame her for that, Mr. Asshole?

The director shook her head in sympathy. "And you don't know where that is."

"I do." One flight and a short drive in a rental car away.

Allyson stared at him for a second as if waiting for more then she shrugged and stabbed her salad with her fork. "But she was just some woman on a cruise so it doesn't matter." She pointed the pierced iceberg lettuce on her fork at him. "You'll remember her fondly and that's that."

The conversation moved on and Carter ate his entire

hot fudge sundae without tasting it at all as he moved through the brunch while in a haze saying all the right things at the right times.

"Oh, one more thing." Allyson flipped through the script's pages as she got up from her chair and then pushed the script across the table to him. "You might want to take a look at this. Really think about where the character is at this point and why he needs to make this move."

He glanced down at the page. "What scene is it?"

"The grand gesture, when he fights for what and who he really wants."

"You trying to tell me something?" Even he wasn't dense enough to miss that.

She lifted a shoulder and let it fall. "Only that you have a week before shooting starts and I suggest you spend it doing something that really matters." She did that Hollywood thing of kissing him on the cheek instead of saying goodbye. "For research purposes of course."

Then she winked at him and walked out of the restaurant. He stood there for a second, uncertainty making his palms sweat. Then he caught sight of the blonde in his peripheral vision again and for half a second—even though he knew better—he thought it was Aubrey. Fuck. He'd be doing that for the rest of his life if he didn't make good on this moment. Allyson was right. It was time to go do some research. Carter was on his phone and making flight reservations before he hit the door.

TWELVE

With the morning bakery rush was over, Aubrey wheeled her new office chair over to the closed secretary desk tucked away in the corner of the small dining room ready to start her new life. It may not be the one she'd planned on having, but it was the one that fit with who she was now and where she wanted to take her life. The past week since she'd gotten home hadn't been easy, but then again change never was. She pushed her chair into place at the desk. It was white with a fold-down top that locked when she closed it, had three drawers, and two cabinets there was plenty of space for her notebooks, laptop, research, and more.

Nerves all jangly about the fact that she was really going to do this, she took out her key and unlocked the desk. Everything was precisely in its place. Pens stood in the mug decorated with the bakery's logo. Her laptop was on the top shelf charged and waiting. Her sticky notes were in the top drawer waiting to be used. She let out a nervous breath. Yep, she was finally going to do this.

The bell on the front door gave her half a second of

warning before the first of the morning gaggle of gossipers walked through the door. Mr. Lucas had been coming to the bakery every morning for years to sit with his cronies and solve the world's problems over coffee and a cruller.

He jerked to a stop in front of her, then looked around as if to confirm he was in the right bakery. "Where'd the corner table go, Aubrey?"

"It's in the other corner now," she said, pointing to the table she'd dragged over to the other side of the dining area last night after she'd finished building the desk and getting it in place.

He glanced over at the table, already set with his usual Retired And Loving It mug along with Mr. Mendoza's Old Fart mug, Mr. Corelli's Life Begins At Seventy mug, and Mr. Jackson's Best Grandpa mug. "Why?"

"The plug ins are over here." Lord knew she'd looked around every square inch of the place to see if there was any other place it could go. "I need to be able to charge my laptop so I can work on the outline for my book."

Oh wow. Admitting it out loud had been a rush. She hadn't told anyone yet. Of course, now that she'd told him, she wouldn't have to.

"You're writing a book?"

"I am." She straightened her shoulders and lifted her chin, prepped for mockery.

"Good for you." Mr. Lucas gave her a nod of encouragement. "I'll steer the boys over here when they come in."

A bubbly excitement filling her, she settled in at her desk while Mr. Lucas took his mug from the table and wondered over to the counter where he filled up his coffee from the carafe that was always on the corner and picked up one of the crullers already on a plate, leaving exact change behind to cover the bill. There was a benefit to having regulars who always got the usual.

For the first time since she'd left for the cruise, she opened her laptop. The screen was dirty with smudged fingerprints—why did she never notice that until she was out in public—but it only took a few seconds for it to warm up and an image of Carter to fill the once dark space. In it, he was smiling, no Iowa farmboy scruff covering his face, as he walked his dog. And with that every happy little fizzy bubble of exhilaration popped until there was nothing left but a chin-trembling sadness.

Clicking on the login button for her Insta account was the last thing she needed to be doing, but her fingers moved across the trackpad almost of their own accord. Her thirst account popped open, showing photo after photo of Carter on the set, doing interviews, and out living his life. It was a bittersweet punch to the gut because while she didn't want to let go, she knew that she had to move forward. She'd had her chance and she'd fucked it up. The best thing she could do now was hit the delete button.

Her hand hovering over the trackpad, she took one last lingering look and that's when she noticed the new posts. That was wrong. There shouldn't be anything new since she'd deleted the post that had almost outed Carter on the cruise. Adrenaline made her hands shake as she clicked on the posts, enlarging the photos. They were casual shots, the kind of fun-in-the-sun photos that the ship's official photographers had been snapping throughout the cruise. In the first pic, Carter had his face to the camera as he smiled at Aubrey who had her back to the camera. In the next, they were on the private island shopping in the souvenir huts and once again only Carter could be identified. The final picture was of her standing behind him, blocked by his body, as she reached around and taught him how to play shuffleboard. She hadn't put these up. She didn't even know where they'd come from.

Heart hammering against her ribs, she clicked on each post, trying to figure out who had gotten into her account and posted them. Even though she knew she'd never see Carter again, she couldn't stand having him think she'd done it again. The bell on the bakery door jingled as panic gripped her lungs tight.

"Crullers on the counter, gentleman," she said as she glanced up, expecting to see the rest of the coffee klatch.

But there in the middle of the bakery was Carter. He'd shaved off his scruff and had ditched the ridiculous Iowa farm boy on a cruise clothes but it was him. Aubrey couldn't breathe. She couldn't think. Seeing him in person was the best worst thing that could have happened and she had no idea what to do.

"I didn't come for a donut," he said closing the distance between them. "I came for you."

C arter hadn't planned beyond finding Aubrey and apologizing. He definitely should have done that because now he was just standing here like a dumbass, inwardly cringing that he'd just said he wasn't here for a donut.

For.

A.

Donut.

"Aubrey." He let the door fall closed behind him and started toward her, having to shove his hands into his pockets so he didn't reach out and pull her into his arms when she probably was ready to deck him.

"Don't look!" Eyes wide, she slammed her laptop closed but not before he spotted the photos on it. "It's not what you think. I have no idea who—"

"I did it." That had been the first part of his plan. "I contacted the cruise ship people and bought every photo their photographers took on the cruise." Unable to stop himself, he crossed to her, needing to at least be close to her even if this might be the last time he saw her. "Then, I went through and looked for any that had us in the background or the casual shots we hadn't realized people were taking. I cropped them down so you weren't recognizable because I didn't want to out you as the woman I fell for without your permission." The need to protect her from some of his more aggressive fans had been instinctual and visceral. "My brother Byron knows someone who knows someone who owed someone else a favor and that's how I hacked your IG feed."

"Why?"

"Because it was the only way I knew to show you that I'd lied that night." *Oh fuck it.* He reached out, cupping her face with his hands. "What's between us, it means something, it's special." He sucked in a shaky breath, everything was riding on this moment. "Aubrey, I'm sorry I was an asshole."

"Language young man," one of the old men in the corner table called out.

"Earl," another one said. "They're adults and you worked construction for fifty years. I've heard you say worse on poker nights. Relax already."

Aubrey looked over at the four men sitting at a table in the corner, watching unabashedly as they drank their coffee.

Then, she grabbed his hand and pulled him into a storage closet so small there was barely enough room for the two at the same time. But he wasn't about to let her go, not now that he was face to face with Aubrey again. To say he was enjoying the close confines would have been the understatement of the century.

"What are you doing in Salvation?" she asked, her hands fluttering across his chest as if she couldn't help but touch him either.

"Begging for you to forgive me." He took her hands, holding them to his chest above his heart. "I messed up. I should have listened to you when you tried to tell me you were the one behind the post."

"I should have insisted that you listen," she said, her gaze going hazy as she licked her full lips. "I just kept getting distracted."

"Because I kept kissing you." And he did it again, pressing his lips to hers and making every promise he'd do whatever it took to keep. "I promise to make up for it—for all of it."

"How are you going to do that?"

Ideas? Oh yeah, he had lots. "Do you have anywhere with more room than this storage closet?"

She grinned up at him, reaching behind her for the closet door. "I live right above the bakery."

"I'm starting to love small towns." So much so that he was already making a mental note to have Byron check out farms for sale in the area. Other actors had places in Idaho or Montana, Salvation might just be even better.

"Me too." She opened the door and they spilled out of the closet. "Mr. Lucas," Aubrey said as they hurried hand in hand through the bakery toward the front door. "Please change the sign to Closed when y'all leave."

"Where are you two going?" The old guy who'd called out Earl asked.

Neither of them answered, they were already all but sprinting out the door.

———

They made it up the stairs attached to the side of the bakery in record time. She'd never been so happy to live in a small town where no one locked their doors more in her life because that meant no fumbling for keys. Instead, she threw open the door and dragged Carter inside. She was ready to head straight for her bedroom, but he had other plans. Tugging her in close, he gave her a hot, brief kiss before swapping their positions so her back was to the closed door.

"When I walked out of the hotel bathroom and you were gone, I thought I was too late." Desire and a possessive hunger swirled in his eyes as he crowded into her space, forcing her to back up until she was flat against the door.

Her breath caught. Electricity sparked in the air around them, muddling her ability to form coherent thought. "Too late for what?"

"To tell you what an idiot I was." He lowered his lips to hers, possessive and hard.

Stunned, she couldn't move as his tongue teased her lips, sending heat flaring through her body. Need and want surged from her core. He deepened the kiss and his hands swept down her sides, coming to rest against the outside of her thighs. The cotton of her sundress felt so soft as it slid against her bare legs when he inched it higher and higher, until it bunched around her waist. The contrasting texture of his rough hands and the delicate lace of her panties against her hip teased her desire. She buried her fingers in his still short but growing out of his buzz cut hair, wanting to touch him everywhere at once. It was happening too fast and not fast enough.

Desperate for more, she pulled back from his hungry mouth. "Carter."

He squeezed her hips. "Whatever you want, tell me. I'll make it happen."

Grabbing a handful of his button-up shirt in each fist, she looked him straight in the eye. This wasn't because they were in a cruise bubble, it wasn't the idea of being with her fantasy guy. This was Carter, the man she'd fallen for the moment he played along with her prank to steal Grace's pants.

"You know what I want," she said as she yanked his shirt open, sending buttons flying across the room.

"You want me to make you come?"

"More." The ache deep within her intensified. Her sensitive skin craved his touch, yearned for him. "I want you. Now. Tomorrow."

He leaned forward and nipped at the base of her neck. "Aubrey, I'm yours."

Her knees buckled and she would have sunk to the floor if his hands weren't holding her hips so firmly. His hands curved around to her ass, cupping each globe in his palms. He lifted her up to her tiptoes, his strong hands on her ass. Using a foot, he nudged her legs farther apart. The cool air brushed against her panties, taunting her heated clit.

Her skin tingled everywhere Carter touched, but it wasn't enough—she wasn't sure it ever would be. Her lips busy with his, she spread her fingers wide and ran them across his broad shoulders. She followed the curve of his biceps, tensing under her touch, nudging his shirt down his arms until it fell from them.

Pulling her mouth away was a necessary small torture so she could taste more of him. She trailed kisses down to his throat, pausing at the pulse hammering there, relishing that both of their hearts raced in anticipation. A quick nip elicited a harsh groan from him.

Pushing her back gently, he framed her face with his hands, forcing her to make eye contact. "I'm sorry, for everything. Can you forgive me?"

"Only if you'll forgive me too."

"So we're even." Leaning forward, he kissed her again, teasing open her mouth with his tongue and then backing off. "A fresh start."

That was exactly it for both of them. A new beginning with new dreams and hopes. It wasn't what she'd been expecting to find when she'd walked onto that cruise ship, but wasn't that how life worked out sometimes. The unexpected twists and turns that lead a person to where they were supposed to be all along.

She kissed her way along his freshly shaven jaw. "How do you celebrate a new beginning?"

"I hear it's very similar to making up after a fight."

"Oh," she said, desire making her shiver in his arms. "I'm all for that."

For a moment he didn't move, then his hands seemed to be everywhere at once. Their clothes were gone in a whirlwind of touching and kissing. His head dropped to her breasts and licked a line of fire across their top curves. Using his hands to mold them, he pushed them upward and sucked one nipple into his hot mouth.

The moment his teeth grazed the hard nubs, Aubrey's legs gave out on her and she collapsed against the door.

Tension built inside her as his hand snaked down her flat belly. His hungry mouth released her breast and traveled back up to her mouth.

One hand slid lower, snuck under the elastic of her lace panties and a single finger sank between her wet lips. Her back arched in reaction to his touch, so pleasurable it nearly broke her. Eyes clenched shut, ribbons of color danced across her mind's eye, their hues becoming more vibrant as he stroked her clit and dipped first one, then two, then three fingers inside her sensitive pussy.

Trying to anchor herself to reality, she reached for him. Her fingers dug into his shoulders, but instead of bringing her back to the real world, the feel of his skin increased her need. It pushed her forward and brightened the colors behind her eyelids until they were nearly neon in intensity. The vibration built deep inside her, ratcheting up with each stroke of his fingers in and out. His fingers twisted within her slick folds, pushing her closer to release until the colors exploded and her orgasm overtook her.

Panting, Aubrey rested her head against his shoulder. She should be sated, but instead a fresh energy buzzed through her and she hungered for more of Carter inside her than just his fingers.

Grabbing a condom from his wallet before he stripped off his jeans, he rolled it on while Aubrey watched, her hooded gaze following his every more. And when he was done, he slid his rock-hard cock inside her wetness, driving deep into her pussy. She embraced his dick, massaging it with every stroke, and within moments he was on the edge of coming. Long, lean legs wrapped around his waist and her round ass filled his hands as he urged her body to slow down so they could make it last. The tips of her nipples rubbed against his chest. Her luscious lips on his throat made him want to forget his attempts to draw out the pleasure.

Her heels dug into the small of his back as she arched back, grinding her pussy against his cock. He slid his hands up from her waist, inching them across her skin and up to her tits. High and round, they filled his palms as if his hands were made for holding them.

Rolling her nipples between his fingers elicited a low moan from her parted lips. Encouraged, he tugged them gently and dipped his head down to circle one nipple with his tongue before sucking it into his mouth. He'd never heard sweeter music than her groan.

Wanting to touch her everywhere at once, he forced himself away from her nipples. His tongue glided downward, stopping an inch higher than the start of her trim bush. She shivered under his hands when he kissed her there, his hands skimming across her hips, pulling her lower body closer to his needy mouth.

Bringing his thumbs to her wet lips, he spread them wide, exposing her clit. He flicked it with his tongue, tasting her, memorizing the moment. Using his last vestige of patience, he savored her essence, not wanting this to end but knowing he wouldn't make it much longer before he had to bury himself within her welcoming pussy once more.

As if she understood his quandary, Audrey pushed his head away and pulled him upward until they were face to face. "Fuck me now, Carter. I need to feel you inside me."

She claimed his mouth, her tongue wanting entrance and her body demanding so much more.

He picked her up, raising her high enough to straddle

him. Flipping around so it was his back against the door, he leaned against the wood. Hands gripping her hips, he moved her up and down on his standing cock. So good. She felt so good against him and around him.

Audrey braced herself on his shoulders and undulated. He couldn't wait; he already had played on the edge for too long. Already his balls were tight, ready to spill.

The slap of their bodies meeting filled his ears and a musky scent surrounded them. Her body, so warm and smooth underneath his palms, pushed him to go faster but he wanted to draw it out a little bit longer, just a little bit longer. He could make it last. Hold her longer. Bring her closer. Make her his. But then her body stiffened and her wetness squeezed his cock as she came. Her orgasm milked his cock and he gave in.

"I was serious you know," he said as he carried her down the hallway to her room where he laid her down on the bed and laid beside her. "You're stuck with me now and tomorrow. I can be based anywhere and Salvation seems like a good little town."

She chuckled, snuggling up against him, her head on his shoulder. "You don't mind everyone and their dog knowing exactly what's going on in your life at any moment?"

"Well, maybe the dog is a step too far."

"I'm serious." She sat up, her body tense and a protective glint in her eyes. "The paparazzi have nothing on Ruby Sue. She'll know everything about you by sunset."

How in the hell had he ever doubted Aubrey? The sun shining in through the window made her hair glow as if she had a halo, but he knew she was no angel. She was impulsive, a pants thief, and had an ornery sense of humor—and he loved all of it. He loved her. And that is what made the plans he'd put in motion for his career even better.

"Then I might as well let her know now that I'm signed on to star in that indie movie," he said, toying with the soft strands of her hair. "Plus, Bryon worked out a deal where I'll play The Admiral one more time in a summer block-buster. Spoiler alert, in that movie there will be a twist where during a battle The admiral is knocked into a parallel universe. After I die in an epic battle, a younger, different version of The Admiral returns to earth to save it and carry on the franchise for another generation of fans. Yours truly will be returning to direct the first installment featuring the new admiral."

"Is that what you want? I thought you were trying to get away from The Admiral?"

"Turns out that I can be a real idiot about some things." Lots of things really—especially the ones that mattered. "Sort of like how I was wrong with you."

Aubrey's nose wrinkled with worry and she let out a small sigh. "I should have told you."

"I should have been willing to listen. I won't make that mistake again. And if I do, you can always steal my pants."

"You know," she said, moving so she straddled him, a wicked grin on her face. "That totally gives me ideas."

And before she could have any more, he pulled her down and kissed her for now, for tomorrow, for the future.

EPILOGUE

Six Months Later...

Outlining was no joke. Aubrey had spent the past month while Carter was on the set for what would definitely be his breakout Oscar role, plotting every moment in her book. She detailed every moment in the New York to San Francisco road trip Alice Ramsay took in 1909 that put her in the history books as the first woman to drive cross country. Then, last night, she started writing and her impulsive muse took over and she had veered off her outline by about a million miles within the first six pages.

"Some things never change," she muttered to herself with a giggle.

"I hope that counts for how you feel about me."

Letting out an excited squeal, she jumped up from her desk in the corner of the bakery and sprinted to Carter, jumping up into his arms and wrapping her legs around his waist as she gave him a welcome home kiss. Yes, FaceTime was better than nothing, but it was still a poor substitute for the man himself. By the time she came up for air—remembering just in time before she went for his pants that Mr.

Lucas and his coffee crew were at their usual table—her entire body was buzzing with anticipation.

"I take it you missed me?" he asked, lowering her to ground.

"Like you wouldn't believe."

"Good because you're stuck with me for the next six months until The Admiral starts shooting."

She sighed with melodramatic gusto and pressed the back of her hand to her forehead. "I guess I'll have to find a way to live with it."

He brushed a kiss across her lips. "And you love it."

"I love you," she said, her heart filling with the absolute truth of it.

"Just like I love you." Taking her hand, he started for the door. "Mr. Lucas, can you lock up when you leave?"

"As always," Mr. Lucas said with a gruff chuckle. "Just wait until I tell Ruby Sue that—"

Whatever came after that, Aubrey didn't hear, she was too busy kissing the man she loved who loved her right back —and plotting how to steal every single pair of his pants without any plans on returning them until he had to report back to the set of his next movie.

Want to know what Benjamin was up to during the cruise? Check out Beguiling Benjamin by USA Today and Wall Street Journal bestselling author Robin Covington!

And be sure to check out the other shenanigans that the residents of Salvation get into in Enemies on Tap, Hollywood on Tap, Trouble on Tap, Betting the Billionaire, and Balls Out!

Bonus!!! Here's a sneak peek at Loud Mouth my upcoming Ice Knights sexy hockey RomCom. If you haven't gotten your grabby hands on the other two books in the series Parental Guidance and Awk-Weird, go dive right in and get yourself some hockey hotties!

LOUD MOUTH: ICE KNIGHTS BOOK 3

S helby Blanton was never going to sleep again.

She should have known better than to watch a double feature about possessed houses while staying alone in a rented cabin out in the middle of the snowdrift-covered nowhere. Yeah, that had definitely been mistake number one. The other big, bad move had been her after-dinner espresso. She was a green tea drinker, but the cabin came with an espresso maker and it seemed fancy and fun and oh my God she could practically hear her heart beating from all the caffeine in her system and her eyes were all, "Blinking? It's for the weak!"

So now here she was, starfished on a king-size bed, practically vibrating from caffeine, and wondering if every creak and groan of the cabin in the dark was actually a malevolent force waiting for her to fall asleep so it could steal her soul. The *tick, tick* had to be the huge grandfather clock—complete with antlers—in the living room. The intermittent hum was the heat kicking on and going off. The shuffle of steps had to be— Shelby jackknifed into a sitting position, one corner of the thick down comforter clutched to her chest, and told herself it wasn't an ax murderer.

Steps? It was her imagination. Or the wind. Or the pipes. Or—holy fuckballs, there it was again.

The noise was coming from downstairs. All of a sudden, the back-to-nature thrill of being in a cell phone dead zone without a landline became a cold blanket of dread that covered her from her chin to the little hairs on her toes. Focus glued to the bedroom door that was open—of course —she reached over to her purse on the nightstand and fished around in it until her fingers brushed by the cool metal of her flashlight stun gun. It wasn't a rock salt safety circle and a blowtorch, but it would at least give her a running start as long as the intruder was human and not a one-eyed ghoul with a grudge.

Okay, she knew the whole haunted thing was just in her head, but tell that to the lizard part of her brain that was doing the ultimate freak-out right now. That was it. She was never watching another scary movie again. Ever.

Slipping out of the bed, stun gun in her tight grip, she held her breath, straining to hear something over the sound of blood rushing in her ears as she tiptoed to the door. Taking up a spot just to the left of the open door, she flattened her back against the wall.

One of the stairs creaked and then another as someone who sounded very un-ghostlike let out a long sigh that under other circumstances would have sounded tired as hell, but considering it was made by a house burglar serial killer, she wasn't about to give him any sympathy.

A nervous giggle started working its way up from her belly. Gritting her teeth, Shelby tightened her abs, hoping to stave off the very inopportune timing of her most hated reflex.

Fuck.

This was not the time for making noise—especially not the high-pitched sound that had resulted in her having the nickname The Squeaker growing up. Okay, it hadn't just been the giggle. She'd never gotten rid of her little-girl voice —no matter how many voice lessons she'd had—and now it was that sound that had telemarketers asking if her mommy was home when she answered the phone that was going to get her straight-up murdered.

Focus, Shelby. Be the badass your tats promise you are.

She had several, but her biggest was a detailed leaf tattoo the length of her forearm. It wasn't exactly a skull and crossbones with a bloody dagger tough, but getting it had hurt like a bitch and she'd survived. That meant she could live through this.

The steps got closer, and she pictured a Goliath of a guy, maybe with a little drool stuck to the corner of his mouth and wild black eyes, walking toward the open bedroom door. She adjusted her sweat-slick grip on the flashlight stun gun—thank you, nerves, for adding that to the mix. Letting out a deep breath, she put her thumb on the switch that would turn on the super-bright light and her finger on the button that would turn on the arc of electricity.

According to the self-defense course she'd taken after the threats got more than the usual you're-a-real-bitch-and-I-hope-you-get-raped variety of being female on the internet, the light would momentarily startle her attacker so she could get in close enough to jab the electric arc into a sensitive spot. The jolt wouldn't be enough to knock him out, but it would incapacitate him long enough for her to run down the stairs, grab her car keys, and get the hell out of this Stephen King book in the making.

He walked through the door, pausing just inside, presumably looking at the tumble of sheets and blankets on the empty bed.

Too bad, asshole, I'm not waiting for you to attack.

Shelby let out a banshee shriek—okay, squeak. The man whirled around, hands curled into fists. She flipped on the flashlight on the inhale as he reared back, and then she shoved the arcing end into his stomach. Technically, she was supposed to hold it there for three seconds. She got maybe half of one before her grip slipped and she lost contact. He stumbled back, letting out a low rumbly yowl of pain.

That's when she was supposed to run, sprinting away from death and danger. But she didn't, not once her flashlight's beam landed on the man's face and her stomach dropped down to the cabin's wine cellar.

Ian Petrov. Hockey player. Curly haired, bearded sex god. The one person in the world who hated her more than anyone else in the world.

"What the hell," Ian yelled, holding a protective arm over his gut as he advanced toward her. "You better get the fuck out of here before the cops show up."

"Did you follow me?" Brilliant question? No, but her brain was a little shell-shocked at the moment.

"Why in the hell would I do th—" The word died on his lips as recognition and something that looked a lot like disgust crossed his way-too-ruggedly-handsome face. He stopped walking and groaned, letting his head drop back as he mumbled curses at the ceiling. "You have got to be fucking kidding me. You? Here? What are you, stalking me? Haven't you fucked up my life enough?"

Shelby winced. It had been an accident, but the result was the same. *She* was the reason why everyone in Harbor

City now knew that Ian's best friend and fellow Ice Knights hockey player Alex Christensen was actually Ian's secret half brother.

When it came out that Alex had known the truth for years without telling Ian, the two men had stopped speaking to each other. Now, the Ice Knights had been torn in two just as the playoffs were starting. It was an unmitigated mess.

Ian may not be a friendly neighborhood murderer, but he might just kill her—metaphorically. All the same, still looked like he wouldn't mind tossing her out into the snow and leaving her to freeze in the night. And part of her couldn't even blame him.

I an Petrov had been in some weird situations with women before.

There was the date who showed up in head-to-toe Ice Knights gear and asked if he wanted to see the tattoo of his face on her ass. He'd declined.

One woman had pledged daily blowjobs in exchange for helping her hook up with stern brunch daddy Coach Peppers. Ian still had no idea what a stern brunch daddy was, but if it was a guy who walked around the locker room drinking coffee that was more sugar and milk than caffeine, the team coach would qualify.

His favorite, though, was Clarissa, who had brought both her parents and her little sister along on their date. He'd had a blast at the amusement park with them, but a second date hadn't been a priority for either of them.

Never—not one single time—though, had he ever been stun gunned in his rented AirBNB by the woman who'd ruined his life with her big mouth and who'd managed not just to figure out where he was staying for the next two weeks but to get there early. He had to admit that before he'd Googled her, he'd never pictured the woman behind Harbor City's favorite hockey blog, The Biscuit, to have a Jessica Jones tough-chick look, but now it was made all the more jarring by her high-pitched pipsqueak voice.

"Look, I can give you a head start," he said, turning on the lamp by the bed. "But I'm calling the cops."

"To turn yourself in?" She crossed her arms and snorted in disbelief. "Perfect."

Shelby Blanton—yeah, he'd made it a point to find out her name after what she'd done—was deranged. Sure, she was hot, but definitely one crazy bitch if she thought showing up at his rental cabin was the way to get an exclusive interview or to make an apology for what she'd done. Standing his ground, he did a quick appraisal. Her dark hair was short and wavy, with one side of her scalp shaved down to such a short length, it would have made a Marine recruit envious. She couldn't be more than five foot six, but even in her one-piece black thermal underwear, she managed to look tough. Maybe it was the tattoos or the nose ring—wait, it was definitely the eyes, big and dark and all but shooting laser beams of fury at him.

"Why would I call the cops on myself?" Ian asked, rubbing his abs that still ached from the quick jolt from her stun gun. Fuck, he was wearing a leather jacket and a thick sweater, and it still hurt like hell. If she'd actually managed to get him for longer, his ass would be down on the ground. He probably would have pissed himself just to add to the humiliation of being held at stun-gunpoint in his own rental.

"This is my cabin," she said.

"Nice try, but I have a signed contract for this place." Check and mate.

"Big whoop, so do I, but mine is legit."

He reached for his phone and she leveled that mean little flashlight on steroids at him again.

His gut tensed, which made his stomach hurt even more, and held up a hand. "Whoa, I'm already nursing an injury—don't shoot me with that thing again."

Getting his ass kicked by a stun-gun-wielding emo Goldilocks who sounded like a ten-year-old while standing in the middle of the AirBNB he'd rented specifically because it was in a communications black hole was not something he wanted to have happen. Once Shelby gave him a curt nod, he pulled his phone out and brought up the email confirmation of the booking.

"See?" He turned the phone so the screen faced his attacker.

She rolled her eyes but eventually looked at it. He doubted it was an accident that she kept her stun gun at the ready even as she stayed out of arm's reach. If it wasn't for the fact that she'd showed up uninvited *and armed* at his cabin when all he'd wanted was to be alone and drinking a bottle of scotch, he might have been attracted. He wasn't going to think about that now, though.

Nor would he be dwelling on his dickhead dad with a wandering dick and former friend who'd spent years lying to him. Or contemplating how several of his teammates didn't see what the big deal was. Or bemoaning the fact that he was off the ice for two weeks because he'd fallen over his own damn feet at a team dinner, gone down like a klutz without any athletic ability, and had messed up his thumb enough to need surgery.

"This is bullshit," the woman declared, but she lowered

her stun gun. "I have the same confirmation." She stomped past him to the nightstand and picked up her phone. A quick scroll later, she shoved it in his face. "See?"

A fast scan confirmed it was an exact copy of his confirmation from the rental management company for the cabin. "How'd you get this?"

"A sort of friend arranged it for me." She tossed her phone onto the bed but held on to the stun gun even though it was held loose in her grip. "Who pranked you with this confirmation?"

"One, it's not a prank." The only person he knew who would find this kind of joke hilarious was Christensen, and they might share half their DNA but that was it. They weren't friends anymore, let alone the kind who would set something like this up. "Two, it was our team PR person Lucy—"

"Kavanagh," she finished for him.

No. Lucy wouldn't. Okay, she might have helped set up his teammate Stuckey and his now-live-in girlfriend, Zara, plus Ice Knight right winger Phillips and Tess had met and hooked up at Lucy's wedding, but she wouldn't do something like this—not with him, not now, and definitely not with Shelby Blanton. It had to be a mistake.

"Just look at this." She grabbed her phone off the bed and brought up the email that had accompanied her confirmation, and there it was in black and white.

> *Shelby,*
> *I know just the place. Peaceful with*
>   *gorgeous views. It's already booked.*
>   *Plenty of space because the cabin is huge*
>   *so you can have enough "me time" as*

you need without being totally alone,
which you really don't want to do,
considering. It's just what you need.
This is actually perfect. Two solitary
birds, one fabulous rental cabin. You in?
Lucy

"I thought it was a joke," she said. "Why would I think it was a bird?"

The muscle in his jaw went into hyperactive twitching mode. "Because we're both a pair of dodos for not seeing this coming." So much for not messing with a man when he was down. "She did this on purpose."

Shelby paled. "Why would she do that?"

"Have you met Lucy?" He shook his head, trying to wrap his brain around this mess. "She's all about controlling the situation and the spin. No doubt she thinks this will fix things."

"I can't stay here." Shelby backpedaled a few steps, clutching her phone and the stun gun to her chest.

Ian didn't need to look at his phone to confirm that it was way too late for that. When he'd pulled off the highway and onto the mile-long dirt road to the cabin, the guy on the local radio had just announced it was ten o'clock and warned everyone to get home before the snow got any worse. Anyway, the cabin was miles away from anything even slightly resembling a town.

"Yeah, good luck with that. It's already snowing sideways out; you don't want to be driving in the dark in that," he said because he had enough shit to deal with without worrying about her stuck in a snowbank because he kicked her out. "You can have this room. We'll figure it out in the morning."

Shelby screwed up her mouth like she'd just sucked on a lemon and glared at him as if he controlled the weather or the Ice Knights' PR queen Lucy Kavanagh. Finally, she let out a very unhappy huff. "Fine."

Okay, one battle won. He'd take it. God knew he needed it.

He started toward the door, giving her—and her stun gun—a wide birth. "Hope you don't talk in your sleep. I'd hate for you to go spilling any more life-ruining secrets."

He could have sworn he heard her mumble something along the lines of "fuck you, asshole; it was an accident" as she slammed the door shut in his face. He definitely heard the lock being turned. He couldn't blame her. The whole situation was a mess. First thing tomorrow, he'd find another cabin to sit and drink scotch in and growl at anyone who dared to cross his path. He'd rather go find a frozen hedge maze to wander until he turned into an icicle than to stay here with her. Glancing at the window, he saw the snow piling up fast on the drive. As long as it stopped by dawn, he'd be out of here before breakfast.

It was a great plan, and when he woke up the next morning to bright sunshine spilling in through the huge window looking out onto the front drive, he let out a contented sigh. This was what he'd wanted, fucking serenity now. Then he made the mistake of getting up from bed, walking over to the window, and glancing out.

There wasn't a driveway anymore. The road back down the mountain to the highway was gone. Everything was covered in enough snow to obliterate any hope of an escape.

The unmistakable, might-just-break-glass pitch of Shelby's voice forced its way past his closed door. "Have you seen all the stupid snow? Neither of us is going anywhere."

The sound jabbed him right in the eardrum and he winced.

His life was so fucked right now that he couldn't even manage to be alone so he could contemplate the dark pit of his existence while nursing a scotch and his misery. Instead, he was trapped here—with the woman who'd turned his life into a hellscape.

Things couldn't possibly get any worse.

About Avery Flynn

USA Today and Wall Street Journal bestselling romance author Avery Flynn has three slightly-wild children, loves a hockey-addicted husband and is desperately hoping someone invents the coffee IV drip. She loves to write about smartass alpha heroes who are as good with a quip as they are with their ahem other God-given talents. Her heroines are feisty, fierce and fantastic. Brainy and brave, these ladies know how to stand on their own two feet and knock the bad guys off theirs. Also, if you figure out how to send Oreos through the Internet, she'll be your best friend for life. Sign up for her newsletter and visit her website for more book news!

ACKNOWLEDGMENTS

A huge thank you to Katee Robert for inviting me to be a part of her super fun, super secret project. What a blast this has been. Thank you!!! More thank yous to Robin Covington, Piper J. Drake, and Stacey Kennedy for letting me join your singles cruise. I couldn't have brought Aubrey to life without the help of editor Angela James and the copy editing skills of Melinda Utendorf. Y'all are goddesses, thank you. As always, the biggest thank you goes to you readers. Without you, I'd just be the weirdo with stories running around in her head.

xoxo,
Avery